I0724527

A Prequel

A VERY JURASSIC CHRISTMAS

CORINNA TURNER

unSeen

Copyright © 2020 Corinna Turner

First published by UnSeen Books USA in 2020*

The right of Corinna Turner to be identified as the Author of the Work has been asserted by her in accordance with the Copyright, Designs and Patents Act 1988.

All rights reserved.
No part of this publication may be reproduced, stored in a retrieval system, or transmitted in any form or by any means without the prior permission in writing of the copyright owner or, in the case of reprographic production, only in accordance with the terms of licenses issued by the Copyright Licensing Agency, and may not be otherwise circulated in any form other than that in which it is published and without a similar condition being imposed on the subsequent purchaser.

Cover design by Corinna Turner

A catalogue record for this book is available from the British Library.

ISBN: 978-1-910806-97-5 (paperback)
Also available as an eBook

This is a work of fiction. All names, characters, places, incidents and dialogues in this publication are products of the author's imagination or are used fictitiously. Any resemblance to actual locales, events or people, living or dead, is entirely coincidental.

*An imprint of Zephyr Publishing, UK—Corinna Turner, T/A

PRAISE FOR CORINNA TURNER'S BOOKS

LIBERATION: nominated for the *Carnegie Medal Award 2016.*
ELFLING: 1st prize, Teen Fiction, *CPA Book Awards 2019*
I AM MARGARET & *BANE'S EYES:* finalists, *CALA Award 2016/2018.*
LIBERATION & *THE SIEGE OF REGINALD HILL:* 3rd place, *CPA Book Awards 2016/2019.*
Corinna Turner was awarded the **St. Katherine Drexel Award** in 2022.

PRAISE FOR *ELFLING*

I was instantly drawn in

EOIN COLFER, author of *Artemis Fowl* and former
Children's Laureate of Ireland.

PRAISE FOR *A VERY JURASSIC CHRISTMAS*

An adventurous Christmas story geared to teens that incorporates the spiritual significance of the season? Can't be many of those. Did I mention it includes dinosaurs? This dino dystopian series is so much action-packed fun, and this Christmas addition only adds to it.

AN OPEN BOOK FAMILY

These unique installments are filled with adventure and Catholic faith. … Joshua's Christmas plans have been altered when he and his uncle take on the dangerous rescue of a large dino mama and her chicks. Darryl learns a lesson of patience and humility when her Christmas plans also go awry. But when you live in a dino-world, you must always expect the unexpected.

LESLEA WAHL, author of award-winning *The Perfect Blindside*

This may be the most unusual Christmas book you read! A dystopian world with dinosaurs run rampant? Yet, somehow it works as two families' Christmases are upended by attacking 'saurs. …
Highly enjoyable, fun series - and this one with a fun and heartwarming Christmas twist!

CAROLYN ASTFALK, author of *Rightfully Ours*

This is the most heartwarming dystopian Christmas story with dinosaurs I have ever read!

RUTH PASZKIEWICZ

ALSO BY CORINNA TURNER:

I AM MARGARET series
For older teens and up

Brothers *(A Prequel Novella)**
1: I Am Margaret*
1: Io Sono Margaret (Italian)
2: The Three Most Wanted*
3: Liberation*
4: Bane's Eyes*
5: Margo's Diary*
6: The Siege of Reginald Hill*
7: A Saint in the Family
'The Underappreciated Virtues of Rusty Old Bicycles' *(Prequel short story) Also found in the anthology:*
Secrets: Visible & Invisible*

I Am Margaret: The Play *(Adapted by Fiorella de Maria)*

UNSPARKED series
For tweens and up

Main Series:
1: Please Don't Feed the Dinosaurs
2: A Truly Raptor-ous Welcome
3: PANIC!*
4: Farmgirls Die in Cages*
5: Wild Life
6: A Right Rex Rodeo
7: FEAR†

Prequels:
BREACH!*
A Mom With Blue Feathers†
A Very Jurassic Christmas*
'Liam and the Hunters of Lee'Vi'

FRIENDS IN HIGH PLACES series
For tweens and up

1: The Boy Who Knew (Carlo Acutis)*
2: Old Men Don't Walk to Egypt (Saint Joseph)*
3: Child, Unwanted (Margaret of Castello)

Do Carpenter's Dream of Wooden Sheep? *(Spin-off, comes between 1 & 2)*

1: El Chico Que Lo Sabia (Spanish)
1: Il Ragazzo Che Sapeva (Italian)

YESTERDAY & TOMORROW series
For adults and mature teens only
Someday: A Novella*
Eines Tages (German)
1: Tomorrow's Dead†

OTHER WORKS

For teens and up
Elfling*
'The Most Expensive Alley Cat in London'
(Elfling *prequel short story*)

For tweens and up
Mandy Lamb & The Full Moon*
The Wolf, The Lamb, and The Air Balloon
(Mandy Lamb *novella*)

For adults and new adults
Three Last Things *or* The Hounding of Carl Jarrold, Soulless Assassin*
A Changing of the Guard
The Raven & The Yew†

† **Coming Soon**
* **Awarded the Catholic Writers Guild** *Seal of Approval*

A Note from the Author

The first part of A VERY JURASSIC CHRISTMAS has
previously been published as a standalone short story
titled 'A Very Jurassic Christmas Eve' in the
anthology GIFTS: VISIBLE & INVISIBLE
(published Christmas 2019).

*So if it seems a little familiar at first, fear not —
there's plenty more to the story!*

1

CHRISTMAS EVE

JOSHUA

Skating gently across the frozen lake, keeping my speed in check, I ready myself—and execute a little spin. Without falling on my rear. Yes!

I'm improving, but progress is slow, because I get only a few days to skate each year. Dad and Uncle Z drove north far into the wilds of Tana State for a Christmas break every year since I was seven, just so that I could skate out in the open countryside instead of inside one of the looming, crowded urban rinks further south. Those invariably sent city-phobic me—wilderness-raised boy that I am—into a panic.

What was it like in the old days, before the crazy scientists and their arrogant assumption that they could contain the creatures they'd bred? Hard to imagine, and

I don't waste time trying. So what if the world outside the fenced cities is harsher and more dangerous than it once was? It's my home, and I like it as it is.

Ecstatic at my achievement, I spin again—successfully!—and tear off down the center of the lake, gathering speed. I love the feeling of flying over the ice, so fast, so free. Out here on my skates, I could outrun even a raptor.

Of course, the rest of the pack would box me in fast enough, which is why the biggest Christmas gift Dad and Uncle Z gave me, year after year, wasn't the fuel, but their time, as they sat up there in the Habitat Vehicle's turret, getting anything but a holiday themselves as they kept watch over me. It was always just the three of us in our HabVi, my whole life—no relatives to visit—so we could spend Christmas wherever we wanted. Uncle Z's up in the HabVi's turret now, carrying on the tradition. Only one pair of eyes, the last two years, but that's how it is now.

Pushing away the sadness that twists in my stomach at the thought of Dad, I bend my knees and pile on the speed even more, my heart pounding with healthy effort. I'm sixteen now, and after nine years I can stay up on my feet real well, but I'm only just getting to grips with the fancy maneuvers. I'm certainly not gonna try to spin going at this speed!

The icy wind whips in my face, fluttering my coal-black hair against my forehead, though I always cut it before it's long enough to get in my eyes and block my gun sight. Yes! This is the life. Okay, so I prefer the milder climate of Exception State, really. But I do so love to skate.

"No closer to the far shore, Josh." Uncle Z's voice startles me, coming from my earpiece.

I raise my head, my concentration broken, wobbling slightly as my eyes scan the snow-blanketed bushes, slopes, and beach coming up ahead.

"Whoa!" I jam my right skate in front of my left one, bringing myself to a rapid halt, heart pounding even harder.

Emerging from the nearest undergrowth is a...yes, a fully grown female allosaur, thirty feet long with a mouth full of razor-sharp four-inch teeth. Uncle Z laughs his head off in my ear, entertained by my emergency stop. He let me get nice and close on purpose, didn't he?

"Very funny, Uncle Z! Aren't you supposed to be on watch?"

"I'm keeping watch better than you, dreamer boy," comes the chortling reply. "Well, she's a skinny, mangy old creature, ripe for culling, doncha think? Let's not look a Christmas gift in the mouth. Bounty on an allo will pay for some of that fuel we burned coming all the way up here."

I eye the huge predator. Same upright conformation as a raptor or T. rex, though far bigger than the largest raptor species and significantly smaller than a T. rex. Resembling a rex more than a feathery raptor with her bare, leathery hide, only a crest of display feathers tops her head. She's thin all right, her ribs showing starkly, but I'm close enough to see that she's *not* old. Or mangy. Just starving. Why? She's moving well enough, and there's no wound that I can see.

She stops at the edge of the frozen lake, stretching her head toward me, nostrils flaring. Close to drooling. Oh yeah, she's hungry.

She actually raises one big clawed foot and places it tentatively on the lake, then draws it back as a creaking boom sounds from the ice. I'm perfectly safe. She's far too heavy to venture out here. She stretches her neck, shuffling her feet, never taking her eyes from me. Having a meal so close is torture.

"Ah, I'll put her out of her misery for you," says Uncle Z. "Stand still until I give you the all clear."

I hear the *chink* of Uncle Z's rifle touching the bars around the turret as he makes sure the muzzle is unimpeded, then the snap of his safety catch coming off. My earpiece will filter out the volume of the shot, so I need only stand and wait.

Something moves in the bushes behind the hungry allosaur. What the...? Surely it can't be...?

But it is!

My hand flies up, palm flat. "Stop, Uncle Z!"

"What's wrong?"

"Look. Coming out of the bushes..."

They're fully visible as they toddle down the beach, one, two, three of them, clustering around the female's stocky legs.

Allosaur chicks. The female is a hungry mom.

DARRYL

"How are things going, Darryl, my girl?" calls Dad as I approach the family room.

"Things are as ready in the kitchen as I can make them," I tell him as I enter, wiping my hands dry on my jeans before reaching up to re-tie my shoulder-length brown hair. "Soon as people begin arriving, we can start warming the cider. Half an hour before, we can slide the pecan pies into the oven. I put the cream in the jugs already and the plates are stacked, everything's sorted."

"Good job. Can you help Harry with the chairs while I go drive the fence early?"

Yeah, I was expecting he'd do it now. He won't want to later, and it's better to check it before we have a load of extra people on the farm for the evening. "Sure, Dad." But my heart sinks. I was kinda hoping that with the catering all ready I could go drive the fence with him, have a few minutes off. I love when it's our turn hosting the Christmas Eve carol service, no mistake, but I've been on my feet working from dawn until...well, it's not dusk yet, but the sun's certainly dropping in the sky. "Is Father Ben here yet?"

"No, not yet."

"I thought he said he'd be here mid-afternoon."

Dad shrugs. "He sent a heads-up when he left as usual—taking the mountain road—but he's running late. He should've come over the last pass half an hour or so ago, so he'll be here any time."

Distress signals rarely make it to the satellite from that winding minor road through the towering mountains that split Exception State in half, and the timid or less experienced driver will invariably drive all the way around on one of the main highways. But it's a really significant shortcut so Father Benedict, being neither timid nor inexperienced and with four-wheel drive, invariably heads straight up and over.

Since it's actually only a carol service tonight, not Mass, Father Benedict's kinda optional, but he'll preach a good homily, and he sings nice and loud. Some folks, like Dad's childhood friend, our neighbor Maurice Carr—who claims he only comes for the refreshments— aren't that enthusiastic at belting out the carols.

My insides clench at the thought of the Carr family. Maurice's wife, Sarah Carr, is really sick and won't be coming tonight. But she's insisting that Uncle Mau bring the children, just as usual. It's no secret, though, that all four Carr children will be as motherless as Harry and I, within a few months. Which is worse, knowing it's coming or having your mother snatched from you in an instant in some stupid farm accident? I shake my head. There's no good way to lose your mom, especially when very young.

"Right, I'm fence-bound." Dad traipses towards the front door, passing my younger brother, Harry, who's staggering under an armful of the folding chairs we use for Sunday Mass. We don't really have any relatives, so other than the carol service and Mass on Christmas morning, we'll have a nice quiet Christmas with just the three of us and Father Ben, though he can only stay until lunch on Saint Stephen's Day.

I head to the hall cupboard to fetch more chairs. It's the only event of the year when we need every last one. Just as I reach the cupboard, Harry darts past and gets inside ahead of me.

"Hey, I was here first! You can't have set up those last chairs yet!" I try to pull him out—he resists. "Don't be so— Let *me*—"

He grabs hold of another stack of chairs, so that I drag him and the stack out into the hall together, screeching noisily over the wooden floor.

"Darryl, are you fourteen or four?" Dad's poised to

exit the house, giving me a look over his shoulder.

"Harry started it!"

"Harry's eleven. You're not. 'Nough said." He steps out and the door closes behind him.

Red-faced, I release Harry. Why did I let his childish behavior get to me? Especially when Dad was *right there.*

"Fine, take them," I tell Harry, who's biting his lip, embarrassed too.

He musters an unconvincing smirk, making out that getting his own way was worth Dad saying he was just a little kid, and staggers off with them.

By the time I return with my own stack he's setting out chairs as though he's forgotten all about it. He pauses to push his short brown hair behind his winter-pale ears with both hands and say, "I wonder why Father Ben's so late."

"Something came up, I guess. Well, he'll be here any minute. Let's finish this and get our afternoon chores done."

Soon enough we've squeezed all the seats we can into the family room, spilling out into the doorways to the hall and dining room, and we're putting the finishing touches to the decorations.

"There." I straighten a big red bow on the front door and put my hands on my hips with a satisfied nod. The farmhouse's steel shutters are all open, proclaiming the efficiency of our twin Renfield Ozone 4 electric fence, and Dad's even circled the turret on top of the house with little fairy lights. Harry, having arranged a cheerful Christmas hat on the head of the little statue of Saint Desmond on one side of the door, is carefully draping the dainty, red velvet cloak that Mom made years ago around the Our Lady statue opposite. "I think we're ready. Let's get the chores done, then we can shower and change and hang out with Father Ben when he arrives."

"Okey-dokey." Harry bounces off toward the barn.

"Don't forget to check on that sick edmontosaur in the handling barn," I call after him.

Although I'm outside already, I reflexively check my ScreamerBand—no alarms have been tripped, the fence remains unbreached and secure—then head to the young stock barn.

Soon, I'm dropping the calf feeder over the side of the bovine pen. I give only a few quick scratches to the eager butting heads as they crowd forward to drink, then trundle the much bigger "milk" trolley along to the other, larger half of the barn, where the 'saur calves are kept carefully separate from their fragile mammalian bottle mates.

Plugging the pump tube into the milk trolley— which actually contains green liquid feed mix, but it's the same consistency as milk so we tend to call it that—I switch it on, then lean over the fence, looking down into the pen—the floor is lowered, of course, like all 'saur handling pens—or rather, the obsoDeck is raised—though here the concrete walls drop only six foot.

"Dinner, y'all," I call. A pair of two-month-old male edmo calves and a single female iggy calf, all three already as tall as I am and weighing five times as much, lumber up to the feeder. The "original" 'saurs didn't grow as fast as ours do now, so they reckon, but the scientists didn't think their buyers would want to wait around. Sure suits us farmers.

The edmos latch onto a teat each, while Janey the iggy raises her flat head level with me, her beaky mouth parted hopefully.

"Just a quick scratch," I tell her, obliging. "I've got to hurry!"

I rub the itchy spot behind her jaw for a few moments. "Okay, enough, Janey. Go have your milk."

I've no bovine calves left to individually feed, but one runty little iguanodon is still on the bottle. I move to the end pen and let myself in, clucking encouragingly until the gangly little male iggy gets to his feet and totters forward as I step inside the safety ring. Only coming up to my chest and being very weak, it's still safe to come in here with him. A bigger calf could crush this little metal rail just by leaning on it too hard.

"Good boy." I offer him the bottle, and he takes the

teat readily. He can graduate to the feeder soon. I don't scratch him as he feeds, except for massaging his chin to encourage him to start sucking again when he loses interest. It's not a good idea to make pets of male stock. The few top quality males we keep as stud animals are always sold to other farms, with only good, sound females remaining here as breeding stock. Janey is in with a good chance of staying, if she carries on growing so well.

Soon, he's emptied his bottle and, after checking him over, I'm collecting the empty milk trolley and calf feeder and heading back to the mix room to wash everything. I'll feed my charges again just before bed — probably with a gaggle of hyper younger guests trailing after me, tonight — and again first thing in the morning, Christmas Day or not.

Reaching the farmhouse again, I eye the empty yard and frown, my stomach chilling. Still no Father Benedict. Where is he? I check the time on my ScreamerBand. Only an hour until the service is supposed to begin and well over an hour since Dad said he'd arrive any minute. Heading inside, I'm checking the House Control console for messages when I hear Dad's farm truck stop in front of the house. He's done with the fence.

"Anything?"

I glance over my shoulder, shaking my head, as

Dad strides into the house. "Nothing. Just his heads-up message from earlier."

Dad's mouth tightens, and he raises his ScreamerBand to his mouth, pressing the talk button. "Harry, get back here and grab your rifle. We're going to find Father Ben."

He lowers his wrist and glances at me. "Darryl, start the…" He hesitates, and I can guess what he's thinking. The hunting truck has a rudimentary turret, allowing better defense, but the normal road truck has stronger towing capabilities. Father Benedict's van is a heftier vehicle than some mere car, and there's little doubt now that he's stopped somewhere in the mountains. *Broken down* being the far preferable scenario than *crashed*, though both are extremely dangerous.

Dad makes a face. "Start the road truck, I guess."

Yeah, neither vehicle is perfect for this.

"And do the safety checks," he adds.

Okay, he's really worried if he's going to trust me to check the grilles and wheel shields so we can get away quicker. Dad always does the checks himself.

As I place a hand on the scanner of the gun locker, he presses the "record" button on the console and starts leaving an audio message saying where we've gone and asking our neighbors Riley or Maurice, whoever arrives first, to finish preparing the refreshments and entertain everyone until we return. It's almost a two-hour drive from one side of the mountains to the other, plus forty minutes beforehand to reach the first pass, though I'd bet Dad's about to do it in thirty. We're going to be late getting back.

My hand trembles slightly as I lift my rifle from the rack and head outside, Father Benedict's bright eyes and cheerful laugh filling my mind.

Lord, please let us be in time.

JOSHUA

"What the—" Uncle Z bites off a word Saint Des wouldn't approve of. "You messed-up crazy 'saur, what you wanna go and hatch out chicks for in midwinter? How'd you even do it? Build your nest near the hot springs, huh? No wonder you're skin and bone, missy."

The allosaur ducks her head to check the chicks at her feet, then lifts her gaze to me again. She's clearly in dire need of food herself, but it's her chicks she wants me for. It's kinda touching. Not that I'm offering or anything.

"She's a good mom, though. Hasn't abandoned them yet."

Uncle Z snorts. "Or gobbled them up."

Yeah, many carni'saurs aren't great parents, especially if things get remotely tough. Allosaurs aren't the worst, but they sure ain't the best, either. "Well, I'm really impressed. Do we *have* to shoot her?"

"So am I, Josh, so am I, but she won't survive much longer without either cutting those chicks loose or eating them herself."

"Well, she hasn't eaten them yet."

"Okay, so say she don't eat them. All four of them will be dead in another week or two. Look at the snow. Prey's scarce; they don't stand a chance. Best thing we can do is cull the mother and catch the chicks. A zoo will be happy to have them."

Chink. He's raised his rifle again. But it seems such a cruel reward for her efforts. "Aw, come on, Uncle Z, it's Christmas! Can't we just catch them and leave her?"

A long silence in my ear. I'm asking him to pass over a good-sized bounty. The Dinosaur Activity and Population department (or DAPdep, as most people call them) don't like hungry allosaurs prowling.

Momma Allosaur sniffs the breeze and begins to pace around the lakeshore, the three miniature versions of herself stumbling along behind. Little carni'saurs like that, they should be bouncing around. They won't last much longer.

"Oh, fine. We'll try it, anyway. Now git back in here before she cuts you off."

Yeah, she's definitely moving to check out the HabVi. It's impossible to completely avoid odors remaining around a vehicle you live in all the time, all you can do is keep it down enough that it's too slight to interest something as large as a rex. An allosaur won't manage to break in, though she could do some damage trying.

Getting cut off is something I take very seriously these days, so I spin and skate quickly across the lake. Momma Allosaur shifts to a lumbering run, trying to keep up, so I pile on the speed until she falls behind. If she's too close when I come to shore, Uncle Z will have no choice but to shoot her.

She's only halfway around the lake's curve when I reach the bank, over which looms our armored house on wheels, with its huge off-road tires, high ground clearance, and full observation turret on top. Of course, struggling up a steep bank of frozen mud in ice skates is slow, but removing them would be even slower. But she's still at a comfortable distance when I let the side door hiss closed behind me and hit the lock button.

Unlacing the skates quickly, I pull them off. Huh, the skin of my fingers is more blue than brown. That'll teach me not to wear gloves!

I scramble up the ladder to the turret without bothering to put my boots on. "How are we gonna catch them?" I ask, peering down. The mother is just approaching the 'Vi, the chicks straggling well behind.

"Unseal a pack of meat and chuck it in the rear pen. Then open the lower door section only."

Yeah, let the chicks come in, but not her. "Okay, I'm on it."

I slide back down the ladder in my socked feet—already chilling in this frozen climate—and grab a scent-sealed pack from the meat locker. It's the work of a moment to cut it open, place the contents in the back of the rear pen and lock the inner pen door again.

"Are the chicks here, now?" I call.

"Yep. 'Round her feet again. Open sesame."

I double-check the inner pen door, twice more—the way Dad and Uncle Z drilled into me from the moment I could reach the lock—and only then press the outer door control, lower flap only, looking through the observation hatch as it opens. A small square of daylight appears on the floor of the pen.

Right. Come on, chicks. In you come. You must want that meat. The chicks should rush right in, too young to be wary—

Momma Allosaur's big head appears in the opening, nostrils flaring. Rank carni'saur breath wafts through the hatch.

No, don't you—

She sticks her muzzle in, grabs the meat and whips her head out again.

Argh! So much for being such a good mother! She'll have eaten that meat in one gulp! Fuming, I scramble back up to the turret. "Did you see that? What a..." I look down, and three little heads dip and raise and swallow as they tear pieces from the meal their mom's just provided. Oh. She took it for *them*.

"Uncle Z..." How can we split them up? It's *Christmas*.

At my tone, he shoots me a suspicious look. "What?"

"Couldn't we... I dunno, take them *all* to the zoo?"

His head jerks back. "*All?* The mother too? Since when were you so spatially challenged, Josh? We cannot fit an adult allosaur in our rear pen, and that's a fact. And the 'Vi would only just carry her weight."

"Nooooo...but...it *would* carry it. And..."

His glare deepens. "What?"

"Well, we could fit her body in the living area and her head in the rear pen. I mean, with her tranquilized and tied down, of course."

His lean, muscled hands drop onto his hips, thrusting out his belly, which is showing the effect of the lifelong diet of prime fried steaks, which neither Dad nor I have ever managed to persuade him to give up. "And her *tail?*" he demands.

"Well, uh...that would have to go in, um..."

"My bedroom?"

"Yeah." The cab "bedroom" has always been Uncle Z's. "Only place for it." I mean, no way to drape the tail up into my over-cab bedroom.

"You know what that means?"

"Um...that you hate the idea?"

"Well, yeah, I do, but it also means I'd have to sleep in with you the whole way to whichever zoo was having them. And the best zoos—most zoos, period—are all further south, so that'll be several days, especially so heavily laden."

That dents my enthusiasm for the idea. Sometimes I can hear Uncle Z snoring even through my soundproofed floor.

"And the other thing..." Uncle Z smiles a little too broadly, like when he's about to clinch a deal. "We can't keep that monster tranqued for more than two, three days tops, without causing her serious harm—or running out of drugs. So, say we do bring her on board with the chicks, then we have no choice but to pull up stakes at once and drive south, non-stop, spelling each other at the wheel, right through Christmas Day and the day after, to get her delivered alive and healthy."

He looks me straight in the eye. "So if we take her, the holiday ends right now. No more skating. No relaxing over Christmas. Just a 'Vi overflowing with carni'saurs, three of them trying to eat our fingers every time we take our eyes off them and the other near-certain death if we get the dosage wrong."

He smiles even more. "So Josh—it's entirely up to you."

DARRYL

I check the time on my ScreamerBand as we swing off the main highway, climbing toward the first pass. Twenty-seven minutes. Dad's worried, all right.

"Start keeping your eyes peeled, kids," he says, as the land falls away to our left, an increasingly dizzying drop opening out to the valley floor.

"We always keep our eyes peeled!" In the rearview mirror I catch the indignant frown Harry throws Dad.

"Oh, come on. You know what I mean."

I swallow and start paying close attention to that precipitous slope below. Yeah, Dad doesn't want to say straight out, *start looking down there for a smashed-up van.* No one could survive coming off the road here, not without a miracle. I make sure to spare the odd glance up the slope and around. Most of the 'saurs up in the mountains are fairly small—well, small to medium— but you do get the odd allosaur or similar-sized herbi'saur. Hitting something that big would bring our rescue mission to an abrupt—maybe permanent—end.

We clear the first pass, and there's the road ahead, visible—mostly—all the way to the second pass. No sign of Father Benedict. Where is he?

Dad drives as fast as he dares, every ounce of his attention on the winding road as he steers into the corners, accelerating down every straight bit. *Yeah, come on, Dad. Faster, faster!* We've got to get right over that second pass, now, before we can hope to find him. How long has he been stopped for already?

Something moves high on the upper slope, like a cloud of small specks rippling across the rocks. Just a shoal of itsy-bitsy piranha'saurs. Deadly in those numbers, though.

I swallow. Raptors aren't the only threat to a smashed-up vehicle. In fact, piranha'saurs can squeeze inside far more quickly.

Dad must sense my churning anxiety, because he says, "Let's not blow this out of proportion, kids. Father Ben's got his priest hole, remember?"

True. The diocesan-issue sleeping vans aren't designed for overnighting unSPARKed—outside of an electric fence—they just give an itinerant country priest a berth any place without a spare bedroom. But, like all the best vehicles that clock up many hours of unSPARKed travel, they have a small, man-sized compartment down in the chassis where the driver can take refuge in the event of a breakdown. Raptors have been known to break into the refuges, but only when help has been slow arriving.

So long as Father Benedict's been able to crawl in there, then even if he actually crashed and the vehicle was compromised from the moment he first stopped, he's got a few hours' extra time. Still...

Come on, Dad. Can't you go any faster? Not that I

want to end up at the bottom of this mountain, either.

Finally, we're climbing to the top of the second pass. Still three more to go. But any moment now, we'll get to see at least some of the road ahead.

There's nothing, though. *Agh! Lord, please look after him. He works so hard for You.*

We're probably God's answer, though, aren't we?

Father Ben, we're coming as fast as we can!

We round several more corners, the last one so fast that Dad slows down a little for the next. Drat.

But the steep bends give way to a gentler curve, the road disappearing out of sight around a shoulder of mountain. More of the road comes into view as we get further along.

Wait! Is that...?

"Dad, something's glinting. Where the road's visible over that outcrop."

"Let's hope it's a windshield."

Yeah. An *intact* windshield.

JOSHUA

My gaze travels to the great frozen lake we're parked beside, the memory of flying over the ice filling me. We only got here yesterday evening. After Uncle Z slept in and we ate a leisurely lunch, I've barely been on the ice for an hour. If we leave now, I won't get to skate again for a whole year. I'm old enough to know that any resolution to grit my teeth and go to a city rink will come to nothing. I love skating, but not more than I hate cities.

I turn to the little family below us. The mother's nose hovers just over the chicks and the fast-disappearing meat, nostrils flaring with longing, but she still don't snatch it from them. She would win allosaur mother-of-the-year award, no question. How can we take her chicks away and leave her? Okay, she'd probably get over them quick enough, but now she's in such bad condition her survival's far from guaranteed, in this climate. If one of the killer winter storms that ravage this state nowadays blows up, she's doomed.

"No more skating would stink, eh, Josh? It's a long time 'til next Christmas." Uncle Z's worried by my silence.

Oh, I want more skating. I do...

But there's a mother down there who wants her *babies*. My mother didn't want me. Hah! *As if!* But that little family down there we can keep together, if we're only prepared to put up with a few uncomfortable days.

But what about the skating?

I glance at the little image of Saint Des hanging over the front of the turret windows. Saint Des, the patron saint of hunters and anyone who lives out-city. Saint Des, so holy he lived with the raptors for twenty years, unharmed. *Don't be selfish, Josh,* his calm gaze says. *Especially not now, at Christmas.* Okay, so they're just vicious carni'saurs. But they're still God's creatures. Saint Des even splinted a raptor's leg once, didn't he?

"Let's take them," I say.

Uncle Z's jaw drops. "Josh..."

"You just said it was up to me. I say we take them."

As a frown settles on his face, inspiration strikes, and I add hastily, "Just think what they'll fetch. A perfect little family, completely out-of-season. No zoo will have naturally hatched 'saur chicks for three months, yet, let alone wild-caught. Talk about scarcity value. And with a dramatic rescue story to go with them. What a winter attraction for the zoo that gets them! We'll hold an auction, right?"

From Uncle Z's sudden intent look, I've finally hit upon a reason for him to put up with this. He always was less sentimental than Dad. In fact, if *he'd* been my dad, I doubt I'd be here, not that I've ever doubted his love for me growing up. But it's just him and me, now, and we've still gotta balance the books, preferably without hiring an assistant to share our little moving home. Yeah, we're happier with just the two of us. Even if that means it has to be the six of us, for a few days.

He draws a deep breath, and I hold mine.

"Alright, Josh. You win. I'll get the tranquilizer gun. But this is gonna be one heck of a miserable Christmas."

He swings down onto the ladder and shoots me one more glare. "And if I wake up Christmas morning with one of those things eating my nose, I'm blaming you."

DARRYL

As we round the outcrop, the source of the glint comes clearly into sight. It's Father Benedict's van, black all over except for that distinctive white dorsal stripe, evoking a clerical collar and marking it as a priest's van. SOS vans, some people call them: Save Our Souls. It's pulled barely off the single-track road into a passing place, a little higher up the mountain. It doesn't look scrunched or bent from here, just parked, but...my insides clench. Long, feathered tails wave from open doors. Dakotaraptors. I count four just from here. Probably more inside and round the back.

"Ugh, should've brought the hunting truck," mutters Dad. "Well, break the windshield, Darryl, quickly."

On this narrow road, it's impossible to shoot through our side windows, and what's a little glass compared to Father Benedict's life? I grab the hammer and whack it into the center of the windshield. Cracks appear at once, so I raise my feet and kick until the whole thing crumbles into little pieces and rains down over the dashboard and into the foot wells, bouncing off

Dad's white knuckles as he clutches the wheel.

Harry's already leaned between the seats and poked the muzzle of his rifle through the windshield grille by the time I've righted myself and lifted my own gun.

Crack.

The range is long, and Harry's first shot kicks up a puff of dust to the right of a tail. I throw a quick glance up the slope at some straggly, windswept trees. Yeah, they're moving. "There's a stiff westerly breeze, Harry. Compensate."

Taking my own advice, I aim slightly to the left of another tail and fire. The tail jerks violently, and a large male raptor with a blue-green ruff backs out of the van and leaps around, feathers flying from its tail as it bites at the injured spot. I ignore it and line up my sights on the next tail. Right now, I just want as many of them away from Father Benedict as possible and distracted is as good as dead.

Crack. Harry's shot goes wide again, but only just. I say nothing this time. He's trying his best and piling on pressure won't help.

Crack. My next target recoils from the vehicle. Ah-ha, a big female, yellowy-brown ruff. The pack matriarch? I try to get her in my sights—take her out and they may all run—but she's too quick. The instant her questing eyes fix on our approaching vehicle she darts behind the black van, calling sharply to the others.

Heads pop from every door—*ah, thank you!*—I manage to hit one. So does Harry.

With an urgent screech, the matriarch breaks cover and streaks up the mountainside toward some crags. Just as I fire she takes one of her species' infamous, lightning-fast twenty-foot leaps, landing unharmed behind the sheltering rocks.

The surviving six raptors race after her, three adults and three juveniles—last spring's chicks, no doubt. I manage to drop the one I injured first, which is moving slowest, and Harry grazes another—DAPdep will have to get some hunters in to do some culling. Then they've all vanished among the crags, though I sense beady eyes watching us. If we put a foot wrong, they'll drop on us like lethal rain.

Dad stares up at the crags, frowning. He puts his hand on the window controls and drops all the side windows so Harry and I can shoot at the pack if they return.

I join Dad in eyeing the road ahead. There might just be enough space left in front of Father Benedict's truck for us to turn around. I glance at the drop and try not to gulp.

Inching alongside Father Benedict's van—there's barely room for a car to pass—Dad spins the wheel and backs up to the mountainside until we feel the thick rubber bumper nudge the rock. Spinning the wheel again, he pulls forward, peering through his window as the side wheels...well, it certainly feels like they're skimming the cliff edge. I try to loosen my grip on my rifle. It's not going to help if we go over, is it?

And then...phew, we're back in the middle of the road, and Dad's quickly backing up to Father Benedict's van. There's a click as he unlocks the trunk door. Then he looks from me to Harry, his lips tightening. Yeah, as the oldest, most experienced, best shot, able to provide the best cover, he needs to stay here. That means Harry or I need to hook up the tow cable. And I'm a far better shot than Harry. *No...*

Harry licks his lips nervously, though his eyes brighten with heroic delight. "I'll do it."

"No, I can do it." I grab Dad's arm, but Harry immediately grips his shoulder.

"I can do it, Dad! It'll only take a second. And Ryl's a far better shot than I am. She has to provide cover."

Dad looks at me and makes a face. Yeah, though it kills him to let eleven-year-old Harry go out there, it's gotta be that way. This is no time for sentimentality. Harry will be safer with me and Dad covering him than I'd be with Dad and Harry for cover.

"Okay, Harry. But wait until I tell you. Just hop down, snap the winch hook into the tow ring and leap straight back into the truck, you understand? It doesn't matter what you see or think you see if you get a closer look at the van. You jump straight back in. Got it?"

Harry nods.

"You'd better. Because one of those raptors could be down here in about three seconds, and you know how hard it is to hit one in midair."

Harry nods again, more earnestly. Yeah, if a raptor comes down here, it will probably end up dead, but it might kill Harry first. Even without a bullet in her tail, the matriarch will be too wily to risk it, but a wet-behind-the-ears juvenile might disobey her. Let's hope she's a bossy-boots.

Dad and I take up our places by the side windows—me in the back and Dad in the front so we can drive straight off—and get our rifles into the best positions. We're kind of having to ignore behind us, but nothing large could possibly come up that precipice.

"Okay," says Dad. "Harry, go."

The rear door opens toward the cliff, unfortunately, providing no protection for Harry. Jumping out and crouching in the gap between the vehicles, he grabs the winch hook, turns and snaps it into Father Benedict's front tow ring. Giving it a yank to check it's secure, he straightens...

A shadow flits across the van. A second later, my eyes find the lethal-clawed shape springing down the slope, wing-arms spread for extra lift. One more leap, and it'll land on Harry!

Dad's rifle cracks, but the juvenile doesn't stop.

I aim, not even taking the time to breathe.

Lord-don't-let-me-miss!

JOSHUA

"I'd say she's about five thousand pounds." Uncle Z measures off the correct dose of tranquilizer from the bottle. "But under the circumstances..." He draws out a quarter as much again.

It's quite an overdose, but I make no objection. I've been so busy worrying about the 'saur family, only now do I think about *my* family. An *adult* allosaur *inside* the 'Vi? This ain't exactly the safest stunt to be pulling.

I try not to bite my lip as Uncle Z waits for Momma-allo to be downslope of the chicks—in the hope she won't topple on them—then lines up the sights on her skinny thigh and pulls the trigger.

She starts, nudging the dart from her skin at once, but the force of the impact will have emptied the drug straight into her system. For a few minutes she stands, shaking her head, then she staggers. After only five minutes, she goes down, but we monitor her for another ten minutes. No movement.

"Right." Uncle Z speaks decisively. "If we wait any longer a pack of raptors will probably turn up and eat all four of them. I'll go and see about winching her in.

You close this hatch and don't open it 'til I tell you, understood?"

I do bite my lip, this time. Somehow, I pictured us both securing her, looking out for each other on the ground, but of course, with just the two of us, one of us has to provide proper cover. My sentimental whim is putting Uncle Z at risk, and if it's Momma-allo or Uncle Z, I'll choose Uncle Z any time.

"Maybe this ain't such a good idea, after all. Maybe we should just grab the chicks and—"

Uncle Z snorts. "Oh no, you don't. Those four are a whopping Christmas gift from Saint Des, and I should've realized that myself. Just try and keep half an eye on her as well, will you?"

He slides down the ladder, shutting the hatch firmly behind him. In a few minutes he lets himself out the rear door, clutching our Utahraptor-sized metal-mesh muzzle—the largest we own—and some chains.

Okay, so we're not looking your gift'saur in the mouth, Saint Des, but...please don't let it bite Uncle Z's head off? Sleek, glossy, bright-eyed please?

DARRYL

Alerted by Dad's shot, Harry turns and dives for the trunk just as I fire.

The juvenile twitches midair, but crashes down on

Harry, its weight dragging him back outside, where it lies on top of him, thrashing. I start to swing my gun round, but the shot could go through and hit Harry.

Snapping the safety catch on with my finger even as I reverse the rifle, I leap onto the raptor, slamming the butt into its head as hard as I can, trying to stun it. No, all I've got to do is...

I wedge a foot against its neck and shove its head to the ground, clear of Harry. It jerks, wild, uncoordinated, almost throwing me off. I've just got to hold it down long enough for—

Crack!

Dad's bullet takes it cleanly through the head and it's finally still.

"Harry! Are you okay? In, *quickly!*"

If he's so much as grazed himself on the pavement, the other juveniles won't be able to help themselves at the smell of blood.

"Fine... Jus' stuck..." Panting, he struggles to get out from under the dead raptor.

I try to lift it, feathers coming out in my hands, but it's too heavy. Dad absolutely cannot come to help or we'll have no cover *at all*. Ah-ha! I drag some of the tow cable from the winch, heave the raptor's head up so I can wrap it around its neck, then press the external winch button.

Whirr...

The winch isn't high off the ground, but it lifts the carcass enough that Harry finally manages to scoot out from under. I shove him up into the vehicle, then dive in behind, swinging the door closed.

Click.

Safe. *Thank God!*

JOSHUA

I keep half an eye on Uncle Z as he cautiously approaches the—apparently—unconscious carni'saur, gives her a few pokes, then moves close enough to whip the muzzle over her nose. It fits over the very end of her mouth—*just*—though he can't use the snap-catch and has lengthened the straps already. That in place, he secures her legs with normal chains, since the padded restraints we use on larger raptor species—which will only fit in the pen when tranquilized and folded in—are too small. We can take the chains off for a few minutes later and see about oiling her hide and wrapping some bandaging around to prevent sores. Right now, we just need to get her safely inside before any scavengers show up.

In between scanning the surrounding landscape for threats, I take a few peeps on the internal cameras at Uncle Z.

He opens up the rear pen completely, stowing the

dividing wall, then hooks the winch cable to her ankles and draws her in. Plenty of cursing as he gets the huge tail stowed in his cab room, and I grin.

Hmm. I watch him fastening the washroom door out of the way since there won't be space for it to lock in its usual position and it's no use it being stuck closed. We're gonna need to hang something over there to stop water going everywhere. Normally we shower every evening without fail—and any time necessary—to avoid the build-up of tasty mammal sweat and scent.

That done, he winches her in slightly further and finally gets the rear door closed.

Huh, so much for worrying about how to catch the little nippers. They've followed Mom straight into the 'Vi. I'm itching to go below. In fact...

"Josh? Get down here and deal with these little fluff-balls! I can't lash this beast down with them chewing on my elbows!"

Great! I open the hatch and slide down, grabbing the nearest chick in time to stop its sharp little baby teeth closing on Uncle Z's posterior. Again, by the rips in his pants.

"Oh no, you don't!" The gaunt baby is about knee-high and squirmy.

"Stick 'em in one of the critter cages."

"Bad idea, Uncle Z. They need to stay real close to their mom or they won't smell right and she'll reject them."

Uncle Z sighs. "Fine, you're right, we'll have to leave them loose. Just keep 'em off me." He yanks another strap tight, securing Momma-allo to heavy rings in the 'Vi floor.

"Okay. Come on, you three, stick with me." They're kind of cute. In an—*ouch*—sharp, pointy way. Their feathery chick scent fills my nose with hope and new life. I get them some more meat and start teaching them to take it nicely and not bite me, an achievable goal since we've got them so young, although right now it just involves a lot of nips from them and plenty of slaps to their noses from me, backed up with convincing rumbles of momma-allo disapproval that make them cock their heads to one side and stare at me. I've always been a darn good mimic.

"What shall we call you, eh? Two little boys and a girl. Hmm." I eye their mother. "Well, *you* should be called Star, 'cos you're a star mom." The crest feathers on her head are even a yellowy orange. "Yeah, and it's Christmas. So that means you three should be, hmm..."

The chicks are downy all over, though one day they'll have bare hide same as their mother. I touch the female's head, the fluffy beginnings of longer orangey crest feathers soft under my hand. "So, I name you Gold." I move my hand to the two males in turn, greenish fluff and cream fluff. "Frankincense and

Myrrh. What d'you think, Uncle Z?"

He grunts, hauling on another strap. "Couldn't care less."

"Well, you should. Good festive names will just make the zoos even more eager to get them. And you did call them a gift from Saint Des, so we should appreciate them."

"All right, they're good names, a great present from Saint Des, I'm setting up the auction as soon as I'm done with this; I'm properly appreciative, really. Just teach them not to bite before you worry about teaching them their names, or our chances of having any sorta Christmas dinner are *zero*."

"I'm working on—*Ouch!*"

Uncle Z chuckles. "Oh, and Josh?"

I suck my bleeding finger. "Yeah?"

"Merry Christmas."

I stop trying to remember how many boxes of ScentBlock bandages we have in the medicine kit, a smile stretching my lips. Yeah, it's dusk now, it's Christmas! And things aren't going badly, are they? We've got all four of our hapless guests safely aboard without anyone—in either family—getting eaten. Star is snoring hard and almost completely secured, and we've even named them! Okay, so it's gonna be one weird Christmas, no mistake, but...

It's still Christmas, right? And wasn't the first

Christmas all about trekking off somewhere they didn't really wanna go, with a baby on board? And they ended up sleeping in some sort of tiny mammal-stock barn, didn't they, cheek to jowl with the animals? With the baby in the feeding trough, which I picture looking something like the little soundproofed box Dad used to pop baby-me in if I started crying at a dangerous moment. Yeah, you could say we're doing Christmas properly this year. Authentic travel and scramble and stuff we'd rather wasn't happening.

Which are we, though? The family...or the innkeepers? Huh.

Well, it's a *proper* Christmas, either way—even if we'd rather it wasn't.

"Merry Christmas, Uncle Z!"

DARRYL

The truck's engine roars as we tow Father Benedict's van—and the dead raptor—along behind us. We've winched the vehicle right up to our bumper, lifting the front wheels off the ground to side-step the handbrake, which is surely on.

"You really are okay, Harry?" Dad asks over his shoulder. "The claws didn't get you?" Although clearly desperate to get in the back and hug us both, he started driving at once. Father Benedict could be hurt or *anything*, back there. Time to get emotional later.

"Fine, Dad." Harry's still panting slightly. "Phew, when that thing dropped from the sky and landed on me..." He shook his head. "I thought I'd had it. But it just wriggled around like it wasn't even interested in me at all!"

"It probably wasn't," says Dad. "Seeing that your big sis had just put a bullet in its chest." He shoots a glance up at the slope, now smooth, open, and treeless. "Right, this is a good spot." He draws to a halt and puts the handbrake on, then eyes Harry and me with the same look as earlier, his gaze fixing on me.

Yeah, we're not likely to get surprised here. Plus he doesn't want Harry to see...what might be seen, inside the van. "I'm on it, Dad."

"I can go." Harry sounds less enthusiastic than earlier, but willing.

"Darryl's turn. Get your rifle and find a good position to cover her."

"Okay." Harry obeys so meekly he's clearly still shook up. Who wouldn't be? When a raptor lands on you, you don't normally walk away.

Soon as they're ready, I ease open the side door, far side from the slope, and slip out, darting quickly along to the nearest free-swinging van door. I slip inside, not stopping to pull it shut. It's as likely to impede my exit as keep anything out, in its current condition. The dusk lighting outside provides little illumination and I peer through the gloom as my eyes adjust. The place is trashed, fridge door hanging open, but no sign of Father Benedict. Or blood, thank God.

Where's the priest hole? I don't dare call to him. A loud shout will carry too far and a quiet one will make me sound even more like prey. My fingers trace over the floor. There! A fiddly little lever, and another, and one more at the bottom. I get them up and slide the hatch away.

Father Benedict! He's there. Slightly younger than Dad, he lies on his back, one arm clutching two books to his chest, the other crossed neatly over it with his rosary looped around his dark brown hand, as though he's waiting to be buried. His springy, tightly curling hair is as neat and unruffled as ever and almost as black as his clothes, his clerical collar making a little spot of white in the dimness. His eyes are closed, his face peaceful. *O God, don't let him be hurt!*

I grab his shoulder. "Father Ben?"

He gasps; his eyes fly open, fix on me. A huge relieved breath comes out of him. *"Darryl!"*

"Come on!"

He's already sitting up, scrambling out. He's right behind me as I lead him straight back to the truck. And then we're inside, the door closed.

Slumping in a rear seat, he shuts his eyes for a moment, his lips moving silently. Still clutching his books and his rosary.

"What'd you bring those for?" asks Harry.

"He had them in the priest hole with him," I say, annoyed with him for risking his life by taking the time to save them.

Father Benedict opens his eyes at last and smiles. "They're *leather-bound*." He displays them, his Bible and prayer book. "Raptors would chew them to shreds. And this..." He pools the rosary into his palm. "Well, I *needed* this. My SOS signal, you know. My lifeline. Worked, didn't it?"

Harry grins, and I can't help smiling too.

"Were you *asleep*, Father Ben?" I have to ask.

He reddens. "Ah, no. Not asleep. Just, er, composing myself." At our blank looks, he mumbles, "I thought the raptors were getting that hatch up at last, is all."

That doesn't mean much to Dad and Harry, but remembering the peaceful look on his face...it strikes me deep.

I don't have time to dwell on it, because Dad climbs into the back and drags Harry and me into his arms at last. We both put out an arm and scoop Father Benedict into the hug too.

"I don't need a *single other gift* this Christmas." Dad's voice shakes slightly.

"Nor do I." My voice muffles against a shoulder.

"Me neither," says Harry, with feeling.

"Nor I!" says Father Benedict—most fervently of all. But after only a moment, he adds, "Hmm, much as I hate to break this up, aren't we supposed to be welcoming the Divine Infant with joyous song right now?"

"We are," says Dad. "Let's get underway, then."

I poke Father Benedict and give him a firm look. "*You* are having hot cider and a slice of pie before we begin!"

"We all are." Dad speaks even more firmly.

"I won't say no to that." Father Benedict's hand shakes slightly as he gives mine a quick squeeze. "*Christus natus est. Deo gratias.*"

"*Deo gratias,*" I echo.

"*Deo gratias,*" murmur Dad and Harry.

Christus natus est. Christ is born.

Let nothing distract us from *that*, huh, Father Ben? Not even a pack of hungry Dakotaraptors. Priorities and all that.

Christ is born.

And life goes on.

Deo gratias.

JOSHUA

With Star finally secured to his satisfaction, Uncle Z moves to her head and raises one massive eyelid, checking her pupil. "Well, she seems to be well out of it. But we need to keep our wits about us. I'm not absolutely positive these chains and straps will hold if she does wake up, or the rings. They weren't designed for this sort of thing."

I run my hands over Star's big feathery crest and down the back of her neck, ignoring the creeping adrenalin rush triggered by her distinctive carni'saur scent. *Flee, fight, or freeze… Nah, heard of tranquilizers, primitive brain?*

Have I ever touched a live allosaur before? An adult allosaur? Maybe not. Not quite like touching a Rex, but it's still a thrill. I shuffle along and, as I reach her ribcage, I feel her gaunt rubs. "A zoo will fatten you up quick enough," I tell her. "And with something tastier than a scrawny ice-skating teenager."

"I'm getting the auction prepared," says Uncle Z. "But start her up and head south. Stop if we get a signal, though—we'll get the auction online before heading on."

"It's Christmas Eve. Will anyone even see it?"

Uncle Z thinks about that for a moment. "Huh. Good point. Okay, we'll have to use that agency. Shame, they'll take a cut, but they'll also be on first name, home phone terms with all the zoo directors and seeing that this beast has to be off this vehicle within two days—or just possibly three—I don't think we've any choice."

"We could take her to a holding pen, I guess."

"By the time we've paid for that, we might as well have paid the agency. No, let's get a deal done while the zoo management are in good festive spirits, rather than waiting for the January blues to kick in and make them feel tight. I'll get a tempting blurb written, anyway, and we'll send it to the agency as soon as we lock on to a signal. You get us under way."

"Okay."

"And take the fluff-balls with you."

"If I'm gonna be driving..."

"Hey, this was all your idea, kid."

I sigh. "Come on, then, Gold, Frankincense, and Myrrh. Keep your teeth to yourselves." I make "come with me" allo-noises as I snag an old meaty bone from the bait box in the freezer and lead them into the cab where I place the bone by the passenger door. Might keep their attention.

No sooner am I in the driver's seat, than Uncle Z wedges a piece of the removed partition across the doorway, over Star's door-blocking tail, to keep the little nippers from getting back in with him. Well, it's open wilderness for the first hundred miles, so a few swerves are unlikely to matter. If we come to difficult terrain I'll just have to shove them into the living area, whether Uncle Z likes it or not.

They converge on the bone, gnawing at it, leaping back and shaking their noses at the cold before darting at it again, but as soon as I turn the key and the engine hums into life, they're looking around. I've no sooner retracted the stabilizers, deployed the mirrors, closed all the non-cab window shutters for travel, and selected first gear, than Gold leaps into my lap.

"Down, Gold!" I push her off, growling allo-disapproval, but she leaps up again. Her head bobs from side-to-side, peering out the windows. "Fine, but you sit still and don't bite me, okay?" Yeah, right.

Off we go. She immediately leaps on the dashboard and runs up and down, jumps onto the seats and generally bounces around like a mad monkey. All the meat she's had in the last hour is starting to kick in already. Her hungrier brothers carry on teasing frozen scraps off the bone. I noticed earlier that Gold was getting the lion's share. Female allosaurs are usually bigger and more aggressive than the males.

As we rumble on and on across the snowy plains into the gathering darkness, all three lose interest in what they're doing. Frankincense and Myrrh curl up together next to their mom's tail and fall asleep. Gold climbs into my lap again and does the same there. I know better than to take it for a sign of affection. My lap is simply the warmest place in the room, so she's claimed it.

I pet her downy head now and then as we travel, crooning to her the way Star would, though the petting don't seem to bother her. The chicks clearly hadn't encountered any humans, yet, and Star was too hungry to regard me as a threat earlier. Whether she would have done, otherwise, depends entirely on what sort of experiences she's had with my kind. Some carni'saurs, even big ones like an allosaur, will run away from you, if they've had a near miss with a hunter.

Most head straight for you, seeing only a soft, juicy meal.

DARRYL

"Oh, here's Mau." Dad smiles under the emergency driving goggles he's donned against the wind rushing through the glassless windscreen, though after a moment his lips tighten the way everyone's do just now, when they think about Mau and Sarah.

I peer over the seat back. We've almost reached the bottom of the mountains, and a big, flashy silver truck is just slowing down and pulling off the highway, heading our way.

"Coming to *my* rescue?" laughs Father Benedict,

from beside me in the back seat, where he, Harry, and I huddle under a blanket, to keep away from the draft. At least we haven't been going fast on the mountain road. "And he prides himself on being such a godless pagan."

"Ah, he'll still come through in a pinch, you know that, Father."

Yeah, rescuing someone is totally Uncle Mau's style. He'll be disappointed we've beaten him to it.

The silver truck pulls into a wide bit of road, performs a rapid u-turn, and sits waiting. Dad slows as we approach and draws to a halt alongside. Thirteen-year-old Bentley's face appears in the back window, peering at us, his rifle's tip perilously close to touching the glass. His eyes find Father Benedict—he says something to his dad and grins.

"Looks like you don't need us two." Uncle Mau's hearty voice comes over the car speaker.

Dad presses our Intercar button so he can talk back. "Nah, but thanks for coming after. Father Ben picked one awful spot to break down, and if the raptors had got us you could have been dessert."

"You all okay?" A trace of anxiety enters Maurice's voice.

"Yeah, we're fine. A raptor fell out of the sky and flattened Harry, but it's nothing but bruises."

Harry straight-out giggles at the looks on Maurice's and Bentley's faces.

"Okay, we *need* to hear that story." Maurice's eyebrows remain right up in his hair.

"Later," says Dad. "I'm guessing we've a houseful of people by now, scarfing and guzzling everything in sight and waiting for some carols, right?"

"Yeah, I'll say. Riley and Sandra are holding down the fort."

"Let's move, then." Dad takes his hand off the button. Maurice is already pulling away, at speed. "Let's hope they've all left some for us," Dad mutters, driving after him rather more slowly on account of us currently being a sort-of convertible towing a heavy van.

JOSHUA

We've been going for almost three hours, pitch darkness has fallen, and my eyes are growing heavy when a ping from the dashboard announces that we've just acquired a satellite signal. I flick on the floodlights and do a quick survey of the area, looking for the best parking location, but it's all so dead flat there's nowhere ideal. By ideal, I mean near trees or rocks large enough to hook a winch cable around to easily right us in the event of getting tipped over by something large. But there's nothing, so I ease us to a halt and switch off the lights again.

Yawning, I shoulder the panel aside and step over Star's tail into the living area, the sleeping bundle that's Gold cupped in my arm. "Have you got it done? We've got a signal."

Uncle Z's no longer at the console, though. He's frying steaks over the burner, bumpy terrain or not, the fumes shooting straight up into the high-powered extractor fan that prevents odor build up.

"Yeah, it's done. I put it on auto-send so it should've gone already. I figured we might as well eat when we stop, then we may get a confirmation from the agency before we move on and lose that signal."

"Great." I'm so ravenous I'm even prepared to eat one of Uncle Z's heart attack steaks, if it's put in front of me. I slide an old mat across next to Star to keep the cold of the metal floor at bay, then bend and tuck Gold against her mom. Cuddly as she is when asleep, she can't stay in my lap all the time or she'll *really* smell like me—not just superficially but skin-deep—and Star won't like that at all.

Uncle Z watches with an odd look on his face, the spatula hanging forgotten in his hand.

"What?"

He shakes his head as though to snap himself out of it. "Oh, nothing. Just you coming in here with that baby critter and tucking her in, looking so like your dad. Took me right back to when he first brought you to the

'Vi." He shakes his head again. "Huh, time flies."

I swallow. Uncle Z don't talk about his brother much. I guess we both miss him.

"Feathery and with a full set of teeth, was I?" I say, to lighten the tone. "Is there something about my mom you and Dad never told me?"

Uncle Z guffaws and slaps his thigh. "Hah, would explain why those chickies have taken to you so well, wouldn't it? In fact, add some fangs and a feathery tail, and it would explain a thing or two about that woman, too. Although, I always said your dad liked 'saurs better than people, but even he didn't like her. Huh." Whatever image he now has in his mind makes him screw up his face and turn back to the steaks.

I'm not even gonna ask.

DARRYL

Dad keeps up the modest speed, but I'm still glad to see the toplights of our outer fence winking in the darkness, swaying slightly in the breeze. It's chilly, even under the blanket, and I'm looking forward to that hot pecan pie. If there is any left. The carols should have started forty-five minutes ago—people will have had little to do but eat, drink, and talk.

Our front door opens before we've even drawn to a halt in the yard, spilling a wave of concerned neighbors out onto the gravel, most clutching glasses.

"Do you think anyone would notice if I just slid down under this blanket and took a nap?" says Father Benedict.

He's joking, but the incoming wave of concern does look exhausting.

"Offer it up, Father," says Harry, impertinently.

Father Benedict just laughs. "Quite right, young man. Okay, out we go." He reaches for the door handle.

By the time I've followed him out of the vehicle, he's staring at his van, a frown on his pinched face.

Dad drops an arm around his broad shoulders and steers him towards the house. "No need to worry about that tonight. Or even look at it. The spare room's ready for you and I can lend you anything you need."

Father Benedict's expression eases a fraction and an almost convincing version of his usual cheerful grin appears on his face. "Thanks, William."

"You've got some *serious* claw marks in that thing!" Harry hovers excitedly at his side. "Are you going to leave some of them in? That'd look so cool!"

I elbow between Father Benedict and Harry, trying to shove my brother away and give him the hint, but he looks annoyed. "*What?*"

How'd we like it if our farmhouse home was in the same state as Father Benedict's van, is what, but I don't want to say that out loud. From Father Benedict's strained look, having his van trashed is more upsetting than he'd admit.

Sandra, of Sandra and Riley Wahlburg, our other closest neighbors, has put aside two whole pecan pies for us, bless her, and for Mau and Bentley too. We're soon sitting at the table telling the story of the rescue around mouthfuls of warm deliciousness as everyone crowds around.

"See," grumbles ten-year-old Royce Carr. "You never even got out of the truck. I could have gone, too!"

"You're too young," says Uncle Mau sharply. "I don't want to hear any more about it."

"Harry's less'n a year older than me," mutters Royce.

"That's enough!" snaps Mau. "It's for me to say when you're old enough!"

Royce is pretty steady and before Aunt Sarah got sick he'd probably have got to come along. But with things as they are with his mom, well…

"*And* I'm better at keeping piranha'saurs alive." Royce's grumble is still just about audible and everyone does a bit of a double-take.

"What the heck does that have to do with anything?" demands his dad.

Royce musters a sullen shrug but no explanation. I kinda want to smile, except…Aunt Sarah. The expression doesn't quite make it onto my lips.

"More pie?" Sandra hefts a serving spoon invitingly, then jerks back with a laugh as six plates appear around her.

JOSHUA

Nestling well down in my sleeping bag, I pull the drawstring tight, yawning and feeling a little smug—and slightly stupid. So much for Uncle Z with his dire warnings that he'd have to sleep in with me *and* that we'd have to drive day and night. Well, we can't do both! So I get to sleep on my own while he drives. Then we can swap. No problem!

I did manage to take a very quick shower, hanging a raincoat over the gap, but a load of water ran across the floor and under Star. We don't usually shower while moving, let alone with that door open. We're gonna have to come up with a better shower plan.

After all that skating and driving I'm more than ready for some Zs. But I manage to mumble my way through a quick Chaplet of Saint Desmond. 'Cos this *is* kinda a risky stunt to be pulling.

The vehicle pitches and rolls, the engine roaring and ululating with the terrain, but it's not enough to keep my eyes open. Not enough at all...

DARRYL

Getting Father Benedict—and Harry!—home in one piece may have felt like an extra special Christmas gift earlier, but it's really mucked up our Christmas Eve. I'm just too tired to enjoy the carol service as much as normal. I even start nodding off during Father Benedict's homily, just like Mrs. Swayle's elderly mother-in-law!

I take care of the bottle-feeding as fast as I can, afterwards, and shepherd the youngest neighbors back to the house. Annoyingly, the best part of the evening is watching the last truck drive off and knowing that I can go to sleep.

Well, first I help Dad find anything poor homeless Father Benedict needs.

Then I finally fall into bed. Ahhhh. Merry Christmas, huh?

2

CHRISTMAS DAY

JOSHUA

Someone's shaking my foot, dragging me from a lovely dream.

"Wake up, Josh. You need to take the wheel."

"I wha...?" Blearily, I peer at Uncle Z as he looks in at me from the little doorway at the foot end of my berth. Heck, it feels like the middle of the night. What's going on? I reach for my rifle quickly... "What's the matter—" ...then I remember and relax. Oh yeah. We're the allosaur zoo express.

"I can't stay awake any more. Out you get, grab a coffee and a bite and get us moving again. 'Kay?"

"'Kay," I yawn, reluctantly unzipping my sleeping bag and shivering in the cold crisp night air. I want to tell him to go away and let me sleep until morning, but I

53

can't. I mean, this *was* my idea, right?

"Oh," I mumble, as Uncle Z climbs up into my bedroom with his sleeping bag the instant I'm down. "Merry Christmas, Uncle Z."

He grunts and the door slides shut behind him. Not much Christmas cheer from him this morning.

A glance at the console tells me why. Four AM, and he's been driving all night. Judging by the puddles on the floor, he still took the time to shower. He ain't one to cut corners on safety. Well, if I can keep going until midday, he can get some decent shut-eye.

Then it'll be his turn. And repeat. For a couple'a days.

This is gonna be one heck of a weird Christmas.

The door slides open again.

"Josh, she needs tranquing at nine. Wake me then."

"I can do it—"

"*Wake me.* Understood?"

I nod. "Understood."

"Good. Merry Christmas." The door slides closed.

I make a coffee and sit down for a moment to eat a slice of bread and meat. Just one. I'll pause in an hour or so and grab another, give myself a short break. I can't shake the sensation of being a porcupine that's had all its quills brushed up the wrong way. I mean, Uncle Z thinks I can't inject an unconscious critter, for pity's sake?

I know he's just worried about me. But it's galling.

But he's just worried. And it's Christmas. I've gotta let it go.

I'll obey, of course. Except where it related directly to me, Uncle Z was always the boss, even when Dad was still here—on account of him not only being the big brother but also owning far more of the vehicle. Disobedience has no place in the life I lead.

But it still rankles.

What, you'd rather he didn't care if you got your head bit off? Forget it, Josh.

I'm trying. Help me, Saint Des?

Saint Des promptly wakes Gold, and I forget all about it as she leaps onto my lap and up onto the table, where she makes a grab for the last of my sandwich.

"No! Mine. *Mine...* Ugh, you little thief!"

Time to get on the road again.

DARRYL

If I felt grumpy when I went to bed it's nothing to how I feel when my alarm drags me from sleep, though I can't immediately remember why. Oh yeah. Christmas Day. Six AM and I have to get up to feed the bottle'uns.

I struggle to banish the feeling as I dress quickly. I mean, the first year Dad considered the young stock so thoroughly my responsibility that he expected me to get up on Christmas morning, not him, I was thrilled, right? It's been quite a few years now, though, and the glamour has worn off a bit. A sleep-in would've been nice after that wild evening we had, too.

Never mind. Duty before glamour.

I traipse downstairs, rifle in hand, and check all the fence readings on House Control. All good. I put my rifle away for the day, slip into my jacket, and head outside.

My responsibility or not, I'm still not sold on the fall hatching. We've always had maybe a quarter of our bovine stock calve in fall and you always have a few late orphans or rejects still on the bottle by Christmas, but having a few 'saur mares lay and hatch their calves in fall is a new experiment. Oh well. For this year, it is what it is.

I feed the bovies, rubbing their furry heads and wishing them Merry Christmas. They enjoy the fuss but suck away, quite oblivious to the special day. Then it's on to the 'saur calves. The two edmos go straight for the teat, but since it's Christmas Day and there's no rush at all, I spend a while giving Janey some attention. Eventually she ends the petting by lowering her head to grab her teat and start sucking.

"Yeah, you have your breakfast, Janey," I tell her. "I need to feed little Mr. Runt."

With a spring hatching, the runty male iggy is the

only one of these calves I'd expect to have ended up on the bottle. That's fall hatching for you.

I take the bottle of "milk" into the next pen, but...uh-oh. The calf lies on his side, his neck stretched out. When I call to him and *tch-tch* encouragingly he just lifts his head slightly, makes a low mournful noise, and flops it down again. After a moment his tail lashes, his feet stirring slightly. Not a happy calf. Oh dear.

I stand the bottle inside the safety rail and hurry over to him, making sure to approach from his back so he can't knock me with his legs. Yes, his belly is swollen. I put an ear to it. Uh-huh, gas. Giving him a horrible bellyache—very dangerous if not treated—but easy to do so. A little bicarbonate of soda will fix him up. The only difficult thing about the treatment is his size—ain't that always the case with 'saurs.

I press the talk button on my ScreamerBand. "Hey, can someone give me a hand?"

No response.

"Hello? Hellooooo? Anyone?"

No use. Dad and Harry are sound asleep enjoying a Christmas sleep-in—or pretending to be. I'll have to manage by myself. Somehow. But even with a harness and a winch to get the calf upright it'll be murder trying to keep the head vertical and tip the bicarb down the stomach tube while agitating it continually. I'll have to try to fasten his halter to the winch cable or something.

His neck needs to be vertical or the bicarb just won't end up where it needs to be quick enough.

Sighing, I fetch a harness and pull the winch out across the pen until it hangs over the sick calf. Strapping the harness around him simply involves sweat and brute force as I roll his bulk to and fro. I step well back before operating the winch. Sure enough, as it begins to haul him up, sitting him on his tail, he kicks weakly, flailing his tail and neck. But then he lets his head hang down limply, moaning again. He's sure feeling poorly. Now, somehow I've got to hold his neck straight up...

"Need a hand?"

I jump, almost dropping the stomach tube.

"Father Ben! Aw, heck, I didn't wake you, did I?" He visits often enough that his ScreamerBand is connected to our system.

He waves a dismissive hand. "I was just finishing morning prayer. Didn't seem like you were getting much response."

"Nope. And I didn't like to try too hard. It is Christmas, after all. But this sure would've been awkward on my own."

"What do you want me to do?"

"Just help me tow him over to the side here." The calf moans again as we move him, tail dragging along the ground, to the wall of the pen. "That's right. Now I'll run up to the obsoDeck, you pass his head up to me and then come up here and hold it while I use the tube."

"Okay."

Once Father Benedict's up top with me, holding the calf's head up by the halter, neck nice and straight, it's easy enough for me to slide the tube down his throat and tip the bicarb in, making sure to keep agitating it until the last moment to keep the powder suspended in the liquid rather than coating the bottom of the syringe.

"There we go. He's going to burp like crazy for a while and then he'll be right as rain. I'll come back in an hour or two and he'll want his bottle then, most likely. Thanks, Father Ben," I add, leading the way back into the mammal barn.

"Glad to help. Even after all these years as a rural priest, I still don't seem to know much about the livestock."

"Well, you don't spend your time saying Mass for the mares and calves, do you?"

He laughs. "True."

Entering the mix room, I put the untouched bottle of "milk" to one side and start washing out the other bottles.

"I counted four 'saur calves in there," says Father Benedict. "Seems a lot for this time of year."

I roll my eyes. "Tell me about it. It's this fall hatching. Dad thought we'd better give it a try since all the other farmers are doing it, but I'm not impressed with the results. We fitted up a couple of barns nice with heat lamps and unlimited feed, chose four calm mares that wouldn't mind being inside for a while, but they can still tell it's the wrong time of year. Every last one of them picked the weakest calf and pushed it out of the nest, just in case. This is the second year we've tried it, but I'm hoping Dad won't try it a third time."

"I don't quite see the point."

"It's all a marketing gimmick, is what it is. You know everyone coughs up for mammal for Thanksgiving and for Christmas Day? But most people can't afford it for the whole holiday season, so they buy extra special prime cuts of 'saur for the other festive meals? Well, when it's born in fall they label it 'fresh Autumn-born steaks.' Never mind that even with what the scientists did to their growth no 'saur is kill-weight in less than three years. They don't have to say *which* fall so people *feel* like it's really really fresh and tender."

I shake my head. "It's stupid. But people will pay a slight premium. But the butchers aren't paying hardly anything more to the farmers, despite all the extra expenses of heat lights and everything, so I reckon Dad won't bother with it again. I think that's the way he's leaning, anyway."

"And fine by you, by the sound of it."

"Yep. In spring, only Mr. Runt would've ended up with me. This is just making extra work and frittering profits away on expensive milk formula." I up-end the last of the bottles in the drain tray and head for the door. "Ah well, let's head back to the house, and I'll put some breakfast on. That'll fetch them both out."

Father Benedict laughs. But when we get out into the yard, he heads for the workshop, where Dad's parked his van out of the rain.

I trail after, wishing I could stop him. "You don't need to worry about that today, surely?"

"I had a few gifts and things for you guys. Some of them weren't edible. They might still be there."

"Oh." No stopping him, then.

"I had the rum bomb," he adds, "but I doubt they'll have left that."

"Shame." My mouth waters at the thought. When Father Benedict is with us for Christmas Day he always brings a "rum bomb" made by a lady to the south of his vast rural parish. It's a huge sphere of rum truffle with a space in the middle full of rum. A sugary, edible wick—or 'fuse'—comes out, which you light at the table. It burns until all the rum is gone and then you can pull it out and chop up the bomb and eat it. And the person who predicts the burn time the closest gets to eat the scrumptious caramelized wick. Fun and deliciousness all in one. Wasted on raptors.

I follow him into the workshop and turn the lights on. The van looks every bit as bad as it did last night, the doors hanging at crazy angles, claw marks scouring it, mostly grouped around the edges of the window grilles. Or where the grilles should be. Several are missing entirely. They probably climbed in through the de-grilled windows first, then forced the doors open by pressing against them from inside, maybe catching the door handles with a curious claw. Like crows, raptors are pretty good at getting into things.

The front windshield is intact, though, which is something. I walk around, eyeing the damage. One tire has been gnawed and sags, flat, but the other three look okay.

"What's wrong with it?" I ask. "I mean, the actual break-down?"

"I don't even know," says Father Benedict. "Clouds billowing from the engine—smoke, I thought initially—"

"Smoke!" Fire's the one break-down that will force you out of your vehicle—the worst, worst possible scenario.

"Yeah, I've never prayed so hard in my life, I tell you. But then it looked more like steam. So I'm not sure if the engine compartment extinguisher operated or if it was just steam all along."

He leans into the front for a moment and pops the hood, then lifts it and peers in. "Okay, it was smoke. What a mess!"

I look in, too, my eyes attempting to sort out damaged components from intact ones under a layer of mostly white foam, though one area of it is blackened and solid. "I don't know that it's so bad. The extinguisher must've gone off pretty quick, right the way it should. Must've been a fierce little fire, though. Look at the way the foam has darkened. But it smothered it. I reckon most of the engine is okay, y'know."

"I hope so." He reaches out as though to start clearing foam, then hesitates. With a sigh, he turns away. "You're right. I shouldn't worry about this today. I'll just look for the gifts."

He climbs inside. I stay outside, since he might not want me to see anything that remains, but when I hear what sounds suspiciously like a smothered swearword I can't restrain my curiosity and I climb in after him.

"Look at that. You couldn't make it up." He gestures towards the bed. "They ate the entire bomb, chewed up the bedding to get every last drop of rum and scrap of truffle—then vomited all over the mattress."

I bite my lip, fighting back a laugh at his expression—very much the disgusted grown-up. "Probably the juveniles, right?"

He shoots me a sharp look. "The older ones might've held their drink better, huh?"

I shrug, still struggling to keep a sympathetic expression. Fortunately he bursts out laughing, so I do too.

"Ah, dear me," he sighs at last, leaning against the wall and wiping his eyes. "Well, the Lord uses all his creatures to teach us. If this bothers me, it is because I am too attached to these worldly possessions of mine. Well, I won't need them in heaven. I can consider myself chastised and thank God I was allowed to survive the lesson. Now, did they leave anything at all, I wonder..."

He roots around in cupboards and under seats so I head outside to wait. Finally he emerges with a bag of salvaged items slung over his shoulder like a priestly Saint Nicholas, looking more cheerful. I'm not sure if it's because of the laughter or because most of his non-edible presents were intact, but it's nice to see.

He leans into the cab again to retrieve the old two-claw necklace hanging from the rearview screen so he can wear it today. We'll all be wearing ours. He didn't used to ever wear his, though he's a right to it—shot the raptor himself, apparently, back when he was still a city-priest—but nowadays I think he feels enough of a country-man to do so.

Yep, even Father Ben's claw-necklace is coming out. It's Christmas, sure enough!

JOSHUA

I rap on my bedroom door. "Uncle Z? It's nine."

Uncle Z emerges almost at once. He hasn't bothered to throw his clothes on so he's planning to get some more Zs straight after dealing with Star. I make a hasty grab for Gold as his soft pink-brown toes come within range.

"You're gonna get bit, Uncle Z."

"Haven't got them trained, yet?"

"They ain't biting *me* so much, but other people? Gimme a chance!"

Uncle Z laughs, clearly in a better mood after some sleep, and shoves his feet into his rubber boots for some quick protection. Gold, Frankincense, and Myrrh continue to eye the rest of his bare flesh with interest. "I wouldn't," I advise them. "He'll smack you a lot harder than I do."

Gold seems the smartest of the bunch, so far, and I'm not surprised when it's the other two that make a leap for Uncle Z. I grab Frankincense and smack his nose, while Uncle Z knocks Myrrh flying. Gold gives what looks near-as-never mind like an allo-smirk when I give her a treat to reward her restraint, crooning approvingly.

"You just look too tasty," I tell Uncle Z, as he gets out the bottle of tranquilizer. "Allo Christmas breakfast."

"Very funny." He begins to fill the syringe.

Star hasn't shown any sign of waking, but her leg twitches slightly as Uncle Z slides the needle into her soft gum, so this is clearly the longest we can leave it between injections. But it's done, and Uncle Z climbs back up to bed, so I head to the cab.

Time to get this crèche underway again.

DARRYL

By the time the smell of cooking bacon and eggs has wafted up the stairs enough to lure out Dad and Harry, Father Benedict and I have prepared a large round cake with a gooey cream filling. It's not a sphere — we knew our limits — but it's a tasty enough replacement for the lost bomb, and Father Benedict's spirits seem even higher as, at the first sound of footsteps on the stairs, we hide it away in the pantry for lunch time.

To begin with, breakfast is demolished in an appreciative silence, but soon I'm recounting Father Benedict's introduction to calf care and he's making them laugh with his description of the fate of the rum bomb — and his bed. There's no time for presents yet because once we've finished eating we need to bustle to get ready for Mass in just over an hour's time. We have to put our best clothes on instead of the normal ones we threw on for chores, and our claw necklaces, too. All the local parishioners coming to Mass will be wearing theirs, unless they've never hunted.

The chairs may still be in place but there're also a million little things to do before local people start arriving early for confessions, including stepping out to feed the poorly iggy calf, who's back on his feet, now, looking no more sickly than normal. Our big family room means we often host Mass on special occasions because we can fit more people in. Of course, there should be almost the exact same number at every Mass Father Benedict says in the area, but as he puts it, "folks are folks and thank God for confession." The good thing is it means we get Father Benedict more often but it also makes things busy.

Mass is peaceful, though, with the children who are too young to sit quietly entertained out in the hall with a large plate of cookies and a rex-robot with the sound turned down under a relay of parental supervision. And then we're waving everyone off—again—and we can relax and enjoy our family day—finally.

JOSHUA

I knock on my bedroom door again at about twelve. "Uncle Z?" I smother a yawn. "Can you take over now? I'm falling asleep. I shall have to let Gold drive soon. She seems keen to try but I reckon it won't end well."

"Coming. Want some fresh clothes?"

"Yeah."

He passes clean pants and a top out to me, so I shower quickly, putting a towel down this time, to try to stop wetting Star. It don't help as much as I hoped. Then I get a mug of water from the freshwater tap and sink into a chair to wait. I've been snacking at the wheel for hours, trying to keep myself awake, so I don't need to eat anything. Gold—who ran away with an indignant screech when I switched the shower on—jumps into my lap again and goes to sleep, but Uncle Z emerges only a moment later, dressed this time.

"She ain't sleeping in *my* lap," he says.

"She'd better cozy up with her momma for a bit," I say. I put Gold down on her mat very gently, managing not to wake her. Uncle Z's gone straight to the console. "Have we had any replies from the agency yet?"

He taps at the screen for a moment. "Uh-huh. Piddling offer from a zoo in Tex State... We'd never get that far, anyway. Decent offer from... Oh, hmm, this one looks good. Zoo in central Yoming. That could be the one. We can make it there in time. Well, they're closing bidding at six this evening so we'll know then." He checks another screen. "Weather's still good. No big thaw to bog us down; no storm warnings. Just steady cold until we hit the lowlands."

He makes for the cab, so I head gratefully for my

bed.

What a way to spend Christmas.

Your idea, Josh. All your idea.

And Uncle Z's never gonna let you forget it!

DARRYL

We're gathered in the family room at last, the folding chairs put away, Harry peering at the sofa as though he'll somehow manage to see through it and identify the source of the little scuffling sounds coming from back there. I'm eager too, though I know what I'm getting because I went in-city with Dad to choose it. I know what's behind the sofa too, 'cos Dad picked it up at the same time, and we've somehow managed to keep it hidden from Harry since.

Father Benedict kicks off by handing out a book apiece. I get *The Memoirs of Saint Desmond the Hermit*, bound in dark blue leather, a step up from the brightly colored kid's book he gave me the last time he was here for Christmas. This looks like the complete, unabridged version. It's not exactly memoirs, of course, it's the official—yes, the word's written here—the official *hagiography* (that's a saint biography, I guess) commissioned by the diocese when they got fed up with all the sensational stories. But the writer had everything Saint Des did leave to draw on, so they called it "The

Memoirs."

We have an abridged kiddy-version somewhere that I know back to front from when I was little. Dad has the full version on his hand-pad but I've never got around to reading it. Now I have my own physical copy!

"Thanks, Father Ben!"

Harry gets *The Tough Book of Hunter's Prayers*, an indestructible looking volume with a hard aluminum cover which is—Harry is soon gleefully informing us—waterproof, impact-resistant, fire-retardant, and even contains a flashlight in the spine.

"Hunters have the coolest prayers, y'know!" Harry is scanning the contents page eagerly. "All about life and death and nature and stuff."

I've never seen Harry so excited about a prayer book before. Father Benedict catches my eye and winks, making me choke back a giggle. "They do," he tells Harry seriously. "Mostly drawn from the psalms, you know. A lot of people in the city don't like them, call them depressing, but I'd rather say real. Which can be challenging."

"They have rather 'real' lives," says Dad. "Tends to put people in touch with the Other, in my experience."

"Did your outfit pray much, Dad?" I ask.

Father Benedict raises a curious eyebrow, clearly confused by what "outfit" I'm referring to.

Dad grins sheepishly and explains to him, "Oh, maybe it never came up before. When I was a few years older than Darryl, Mau and I ran off to work in a HabVi for a season. But only one season. I won't lie, it was even harder and more dangerous work than farming, and nowhere near as glamorous as we'd hoped, and we soon came home again with our tails somewhat between our legs—which Riley has never let us forget."

I grin at his rueful expression. I've no desire to run off to work in a HabVi, the way a lot of farmboys do—but I've even less desire to run off to the city, the other common destination for restless young farmboys—and girls.

"It sure is a tough life, from what I've seen," says Father Benedict. "I used to minister at the 'Vi-park as much as I could, back when I was still a city-priest, and I still run into hunters occasionally as I travel around. They don't deserve their bad rep, for the most part."

"Yeah," agrees Dad. "I'm not sorry we did it, not at all. We grew more backbone in those few months than in the rest of our lives. And something even more important—we came back appreciating what we had. No money will buy that. Oh, but"—he glances at me—"in answer to your question, Darryl, they didn't all gather round every evening and pray, if that's what you mean. But there was prayer everywhere, just thrown in during normal talk, in danger and at rest. They believed all right. In something, anyway. They didn't often talk to God directly in that 'Vi, just Saint Desmond."

"Via a saint is better than not talking to God at all," says Father Benedict. "Though they sure are prone to taking it to extremes, some of them. Still, many people are too quick to knock Saint Desmond. The good influence he exercises on hunter culture is immense. You know how much their customs aim to avoid conflict—above all within an outfit but also between different HabVis. Doesn't always work, you get fights and scuffles and vendettas, of course, but they certainly wouldn't do half as well as they do without Saint Des."

"That's certainly true," says Dad. "I've seen hard-as-nails hunters turn their back and walk away from an insult that would turn your hair blue all because they're not prepared to make Saint Des mad."

"Because Saint Desmond was completely against fighting or violence of any kind," says Father Benedict nodding and smiling, "rather like Saint Francis of Assisi. Yet he lived in his cave, in raptor territory, without any fence to protect him, so who would ever dare call him a coward—or those with devotion to him?"

Hopefully Harry will lend me his book sometime. City-folk lump farmers and hunters together, but while we sure know a lot more about hunters than city-folk do, they're a mystery to us too, in many ways. They face a lot of prejudice from snooty city-folk—far more than we do—and it makes them keep to themselves.

Father Benedict hands Dad his gift—which turns out to be *The Working Man's Prayer Diary*, which he seems pleased with—then he describes the candy he'd intended to give us with the books. But we're all too pleased with our gifts to feel sad.

"I'm sure the raptors enjoyed the candy as much as we would've done," I assure Father Benedict, making him laugh.

"Probably more!" says Harry. "Bet they'd never tasted it before!"

We present Father Benedict with the quilt the local Catholic Women's Group has made for his van, which he clearly appreciates even more than he would've done before all his bedding got shredded. After a quick family confab after Mass, Harry and I are able to give Father Benedict the two new sheet and pillowcase sets Dad brought back from the city for us, neither of which we've unpacked yet. They're both an identical pattern of small 'saur footprints interspersed with flowers and buds, Harry's in orangey-brown and mine in dark blue. Fun but not childish. Father Benedict seems to like them, anyway. Though anything's better than vomity rags, I guess.

"We'll find everything else you need to tide you over," says Dad, once we've given Father Benedict more planned presents such as chocolate liqueurs and licorice. "But no need to worry about all that now."

More scratching sounds from behind the sofa have Harry staring in eager suspicion, but Dad brings out my present next—a new rifle. I've been starting to seriously outgrow mine. This should do me for several years, though I might need another once I stop growing.

Only then does Dad bring out a small covered cage from behind the sofa and give it to Harry. He whips the cover off, revealing a leggy, feather-less little carni'saur about twelve inches tall, most of it thin neck and legs, with tiny head and a long, whippy tail. A piranha'saur.

"Thanks, Dad!"

Dad grins. "Well, better luck this time."

"Huh." Harry gives me a dirty look, and Father Benedict winces. The kitten Father Benedict was responsible for choosing for me many years ago grew into a psychotic super-hunter that has already killed Harry's previous two pet piranha'saurs, despite piranha'saurs being feisty little devils that rarely fall victim to cats. "Can't you teach that thing to leave piranha'saurs alone?" Harry demands.

"How, Harry? I did try. I even offered to shoot it, but Dad won't let me 'cos it keeps down the vermin so well. If you've any fresh ideas..."

Harry shrugs and turns his attention to his new pet. The little 'saur stares at him as he peers in at it, pre-tamed enough to be unafraid of him but not yet safe to handle without getting nipped.

"You might want these." I hand him a gift-wrapped package.

He unfastens the reusable sheet of wrapping to reveal a selection of bags of tiny piranha'saur-sized training treats and a new leash and harness to help with exercising until it's completely tamed.

"Thanks, Ryl!" He opens a packet immediately and drops a treat through the bars. "See, I'm your friend. I'm the one you don't nip. Here you go..."

Anticipating many future little nips to *my* ankles, I sigh, then catch Dad doing the same. We exchange a look and try not to laugh. Harry's too busy with his new pet to notice, so I start to show off my rifle to Father Benedict, pointing out the best features. Father Benedict may be a city-man, born and bred, but he's been a rural priest long enough to have developed a healthy interest in good quality firearms, even though he doesn't actually carry any around with him, so I don't think he's feigning interest. If he seems a little distracted, he's probably thinking about his van.

Dad knows all about my new rifle already, and soon he breaks things up and gets us all fixing lunch while he heads to the console and starts sending and answering some mysterious messages he closes if anyone gets too close. What's he up to?

I forget about it quickly enough as we stuff ourselves with lamb, potatoes, stuffing, gravy-soaked cabbage, an entire edmo egg scrambled with onions and bacon, and all the other festive favorites. The piranha'saur sits by Harry's plate in its little cage, gobbling tiny bits of whatever Harry has on his plate while Harry runs through various possible names. Yep, it'll soon bond with Harry, now he's the one feeding it. The cat is too savage to be allowed in the house anymore, so the little critter will be safe inside, at least.

When it comes to dessert I find myself feeling a little grumpy again—I really do look forward to that bomb. It's a stupid thing to get in a mood about, though, so I smile and laugh, and Dad and Harry's delight when we bring out the unexpected cake-substitute makes it almost better than if we had the real thing. Almost. I can't help licking my lips at the thought of the real thing.

Father Benedict looks pleased too—but still a little strained. I guess it takes a lot to make up for having your home trashed like that. And I'm moping about some big cake?

Snap out of it, Darryl.

Poor Father Ben. I wish there was something we could do.

JOSHUA

There's knocking on my bedroom door. "Josh, your turn to drive."

Sleepily, I sit up and stretch to touch the control panel by the door. Nine PM. "Coming," I yawn, reaching for my sweater. Most hunters sleep clothed, ready for anything, Uncle Z's just weird. Always has been.

I jump down quickly. Uncle Z's waiting, bleary-eyed and with several new bandages on his fingers. "How'd the auction go?" I ask.

"The Yoming zoo won it. I had them cancel the bids that were too far away, but Yoming was second highest anyway. I plotted a course that should get us there in time, keep us on that unless there's a big problem. They've just issued a general storm warning for the whole of Tana state, but we're heading south so hopefully we'll stay ahead of anything that develops. And I've tranqued her again, so she should be good for at least another eight hours. You'll need to sleep by then, so just wake me, okay?"

I nod. "'Kay. Is something wrong with the shower?"

Uncle Z shakes his head, but he looks dry. "We're getting that emaciated allo too wet. And I think we'd better save every minute we can. We can skip a few showers. We just don't have anything like as much tranquilizer as I'd like."

"Okay." We've got these tasty little chicks in here, after all, so there's only so much we can do about tempting smells. The ScentBlock mister in the living area will be helping to cloak odors, anyway, though it's better not to rely on it.

"Right. I'm gonna hit the sack."

"Merry Christmas," I say once more, since it'll be tomorrow by the time he's awake again.

His lip quirks, but he just says, "Merry Christmas," and disappears up into the bedroom.

Right, time for a snack and off we go. Again. I check the console. We'll reach Yoming Central Zoo around noon the day after tomorrow, all going well. I think of the massive doses of tranquilizers we've been putting into Star. Heck, Uncle Z's right, we'll be almost out by then, surely? Sandwich in hand, I head for the driver's seat.

No hanging around.

3

SAINT STEPHEN'S DAY

DARRYL

I wake with a gradual sense that something isn't quite right. Or is different, anyway. It feels like—I glance at the clock glowing on my bedside table—yes, one AM, the middle of the night. I lie still for a moment, listening hard. Finally, I hear a faint metallic sound from outside. What? I slip out of bed, grab my rifle from underneath it and head to the window, touching the control panel to open the shutters a crack.

The yard is empty. But there's another faint noise from the direction of the workshop. I peer in that direction, but with the angle from the farmhouse I can barely see it. Who on earth would be in there at this time? Have we got...thieves? For real? Surely not. Has an animal got in? It must be trashing the place if we can hear things falling over from here.

I'd better tell Dad. Slinging my rifle over my shoulder, I open the door and tip-toe along to Dad's room, letting myself in without knocking. No need to wake everyone unless we have to.

"Dad?" I flick the light on, but his bed is empty. What? Is it Dad in the workshop? Or has he already heard the noises and gone to investigate? Alone? Is that a good idea? What if it *is* thieves? Or a large critter?

I hurry downstairs and slip out the back door so I can approach from the rear of the workshop. I haul myself up on top of the outhouse and look through the workshop's high, reinforced, raptor-proof window.

What the—?

The lights are all on. Father Benedict's van is high up on the jacks. And there's Dad. And Uncle Mau. And Riley. And several other male parishioners. Petite Mrs. Swayle, our third closest neighbor, somewhat older than Dad and Mau and Riley, is bending over the engine, which has been winched out and placed in the engine work-cradle. Well, there isn't a thing *she* doesn't know about engines. Mau's in one corner welding up a detached door, everyone walking wide of the cascading sparks. Are they...are they trying to *fix* it? All in one night, as a surprise belated Christmas present?

I press my hands hard against the wall, delighted. What a wonderful idea! Why didn't Dad bring me in on it, though? I can help!

But you've got to get up at six, grumbles a sour little voice in my head. *And you didn't even get to sleep in this morning. Is this really how you want to spend your Christmas night?*

Pushing the little voice away, I try to ignore it. I've been wishing I could do something for Father Benedict, and now I can!

I let myself back down to the ground, my rifle scraping slightly against the outhouse roof, and hurry around to the workshop door. When I open it and step inside they all freeze and look around in alarm. Tina Swayle smiles when she sees it's me and bends over the engine again, a large wrench in her small hand. Everyone else sighs and shakes their heads and grins sheepishly.

"Dad, are you fixing the van?" I hurry over to where he's snipping out a big chunk of badly damaged wheel arch with a large pair of mechanical cutters. "Can I help?"

"Oh, Darryl, I'm sorry we woke you, when you have to get up to deal with the calves and all."

He's given me the perfect excuse to go back to bed, but… "I want to help anyway!"

"Well…it's up to you. Can you get started on the interior? Get the cupboard doors back on, tidy up, that sort of thing?"

"Sure." I put my rifle by the workshop door, out of the way, and climb up into the van eagerly, then climb straight back down again to fetch a work light. The battery is disconnected, even assuming no wiring got gnawed. I'd better check that.

First, I simply clean. All the ruined stuff into garbage bags and tossed out, except a few things I'll check if Father Benedict wants. The mattress is going to be one of the biggest problems. The foam is badly torn up, not to mention the vomit. Actually, we've got an airbed for sleepovers. We can lend him that. It's only until he can get in-city and fix it up properly. Though knowing Father Benedict, he'll want to meet as many of his Christmas week commitments as he can and only then take the time.

But yeah, the air mattress will do. This one's past saving. I drag the stinking thing out and dump it beside the garbage bags.

Once everything's clean I can start actually fixing stuff. Two of the cupboard doors simply screw back on; the third is badly splintered around the hinge, so I have to add some reinforcement before putting it back on.

Dad looks in as I'm checking the fridge. "Wow, this is better already."

"Yep, it sure helps just to get rid of the mess. The fridge is okay, but the pin that holds the door shut is gone. Can you make another?"

"I'll get Riley on it; he's good at that sort of thing."

The van rocks as Uncle Mau starts reattaching a door. It's particularly good of him to be here, what with Sarah and all. I guess she's sound asleep, but still. I give him a grin and he grins back more cheerfully than usual just now. Maybe it's taking his mind off things.

There's no doubt the van is going to look much the worse for wear, but it's still amazing how fast it's coming together. I guess if this crowd can't fix it up in one night, then it can't be done.

Right, time for a wiring inspection. Then I'll see if I can sew some patches over the torn seats. And maybe find some throws to go over, make them look nice again. First, though—I glance around at the busy workshop and check the time: four AM—first I'll tip-toe back into the house and bring out some refreshments. Everyone must be parched and famished by now.

I'd better be very quiet. The guestroom is at the back of the house so Father Benedict won't have heard a thing. I'd hate to blow that now.

JOSHUA

The engine bellows as we climb another incline. I check the terrain map, ensuring I'm still following the best course. Or what's probably the best course. You never know until you get there, off-road. Landscapes change, rocks fall, rivers flood or shift. That's why you keep your eyes open.

And why, as a general rule, you don't drive at night. But we ain't got much choice right now. We've gotta get Star to that zoo within the next thirty hours or so, or we'll have to put her out of the 'Vi and let her go—which might be tricky if we leave it too late and she's waking up. We could still take the chicks to safety, of course, but with her sale agreed and after all this trouble to keep them together, it sure would be disappointing, especially if we ended up having to shoot her after all.

A yawn cracks my jaws and I flex my stiff hands on the wheel, shifting my shoulders in the roll-harness. Driving along with just a lap belt on a clear day in flat country's all very well, but if Uncle Z saw me without the harness just now—"That thing ain't decorative, Josh." Dad used to be real scathing about hunters who'd never forget their safety catch but would ignore their harness.

Every muscle's stiffening up. Should I stop for a quick break? I've been driving for over seven hours. But it's not long since I paused to feed that big lump of meat to Gold and her brothers, hoping to settle them off to sleep again. Hope fulfilled—Frankie and Myrrh are curled up beside mom's tail and Gold has insisted on settling back into my warm lap. She's got strong survival instincts, that one. She makes a nice, feathery lap warmer, so win-win.

No, I'd better keep going a bit longer. At five I'll wake Uncle Z and go to bed.

The headlights make the rocks at the top of the slope glow pale in the darkness. I peer at them. Yep, we came through here on the way. Mebbe another eleven hours off-road and we'll reach the main highway that cuts across the top of Exception State and into Yoming. We'll make five times better time, then; should reach the zoo in about another nine hours.

We may be able to use a few minor roads to speed our off-road leg but at this time of year they're invisible under the snow and once we get into warmer, lower elevation terrain they're often such muddy quagmires it's quicker to stay off-road entirely. We'll see.

If I recollect, there's a flat valley at the bottom here, followed by some stony ground we should make good time on. I shift into a lower gear as we start to descend, alert to every slip and slide of the vehicle under me. But we're gripping okay. No smooth ice. Soon we're at the bottom and rolling over snowy grassland.

I remember this reedy stretch. In fact, there are our tire marks from the way out, frozen and preserved. I adjust course to stay safely on top of them. There's been no rain or snow, so the ground should be just the same.

Little creaky vibrations are coming through the steering wheel, though. The vehicle shudders ominously under me. The frozen wet ground is threatening to give way under us. I shift down and press the accelerator, trying to increase our speed as gently as possible and get us over the dodgy surface as quick I can. Reeds flash past. Heck, this was fine the other day! Why's it feel so red-line now?

Ah, outage! I don't take my eyes from the tire tracks to glance at the huge leathery tail lying beside the driver's seat, but... *Star*. She weighs two and a half tons. We were already carrying a normal load of supplies and gear, add her, and...

Reeds, still. How far did this wet area extend? Should I try and turn back? No...the ice still shudders under us, only our increased speed is getting us over it safely. We can't stop. This fence has gone live; all we can do is get across as fast as possible.

Gold stirs in my lap, raising her head. Can she sense my unease?

"Go to sleep, Gold," I murmur, adding a few reassuring allo-noises. I don't want her distracting me.

Fortunately, she can't see anything dangerous, so

she puts her head back down and obliges me.

Dimly, some way ahead, I begin to make out the other side of the valley. Nearly there. *Come on, come on...* I'm driving faster than is safe in the dark, but not as fast as I'd like in the circumstances. *Come on, come on...*

Crackle-crack-crackle...

The front wheels plunge through the frozen surface of the marsh.

DARRYL

When I return to the workshop lugging a thermos of coffee, another of tea, and a large cooler full of hot pie and leftover-Christmas-dinner sandwiches everyone falls on my offerings like ravenous raptors. I heated everything up with the kitchen door tight closed and the window open to avoid delicious aromas waking Father Benedict, then left through the back door again, but people haven't been munching long when Harry slips into the workshop, looking confused and excited.

"Yo, what the heck is happening?" Eagerly he grabs a sandwich. "Are you having a private Christmas party?"

Everyone laughs.

"You could call it that," says Uncle Mau. "Seeing that it's Christmas."

"It's a *work* party," Dad explains. "We're fixing up

Father Ben's van, secret-like."

"Awesome! Why didn't you wake me?"

"Oh, something about not wanting you all grumpy tomorrow when there are chores to be done," says Dad dryly.

Harry sniffs and looks offended. "I'm not some little kid!"

"I guess not," agrees Dad. "Since you're up, can you put a new tire on that wheel?"

"Sure, but do we have one that small?"

"Tina had one and brought it over." Dad points.

Harry crams the remains of his sandwich into his mouth all at once and rushes to begin the task as though still afraid of being sent back to bed. I stay sitting on a work table and finish my snack more slowly. I'm starting to know I've been up and working since one AM. I could plead calf-feeding and go to bed…

No, I'm not quitting. We've only got a couple of hours to finish this. I lick my fingers clean and climb back up into the vehicle.

JOSHUA

The roll harness slams the breath from me as I'm flung forward—my wild grab just manages to catch Gold, but screeches of pain and alarm come from the floor as the other chicks are tumbled forwards.

I wait, gasping for air, as the vehicle settles slightly. Are the back wheels gonna go through? We're not gonna sink entirely—ain't that kind of marsh. Wetland, really, but all four wheels through the frozen crust is far worse than just two.

I feel the creaking vibrations through the wheel more than hear it with my ears, but it quiets down without the rear wheels dropping. Gold twists free and bolts into the living area, running to her mother, and the other two follow her, scared but hopefully uninjured. Heck, has this woken Star? It *shouldn't've...*

Her tail remains still, so I unfasten the harness and wrap my arms around my aching chest. *Owwwww.*

"Josh?" Uncle Z's there beside me, gripping his rifle, peering through the windscreen. "What's happening? You okay? Do we need the rex gun?"

"Nothing's attacking us," I reassure him. "We broke through the surface of the marsh. I'm so sorry, Uncle Z! I thought if we followed our own tracks we'd be okay— but I didn't think about Star until it was too late to go back. Now we're—" I gesture, then wince.

"Never mind. What's wrong with your chest?"

"It's just—" I try to stop cradling my ribs. "Just bruises, I think. You okay?"

"Me? Sure. That's why the front bulkhead's padded, right?"

"Yeah. What are we gonna do?"

Uncle Z peers out at the frozen reeds and the darkness. "Well, it ain't light for four hours. So I'm gonna stick that Christmas dinner we never ate in to cook while you get some Zs. We'll eat it in a few hours, just before it gets light, then we'll see about extracting ourselves. What else can we do?"

I hang my head. What else. Nothing. We can't do a recovery in the dark. It would be suicide. My stupid mistake has cost us five, six hours driving time, easily. Can we even make it to the zoo in time, now?

"I'm real sorry, Uncle Z—"

He squeezes my shoulder. "The 'Vi's coping with the extra weight so well it just don't affect the handling as much as I'd've expected. It might've caught me out too, Josh. Who knows? It's done. And if it were a proper lake you'd never have driven out onto it without thinking about weight; no way, Hosea. Go to bed. No, let me see those ribs first."

I follow him into the back. The chicks are cowering in the gap between Star and the wall, flat to the floor. I make the sort of *come here, all's well* noises Star would make to them if they'd been hiding somewhere, waiting for her to return, and they peep out at me. When I crouch down—wincing—and back up the allo-speak with the offer of treats, Gold is over to me in an instant, the other two not far behind. I croon soothingly to them as I check their little limbs and tails and necks. "Yeah, they're okay."

"Good. Let's see the damage."

As Uncle Z pokes my ribs I'm too busy clenching my teeth together to speak. But once he diagnoses bruising and a possible crack in the one that made me flinch the most, I finally dare to ask, "Have we got enough tranquilizers for Star, Uncle Z?"

He grimaces. "We'll have to space out the injections a bit further. Mebbe give a lower dose more often, but overall make it less, and give her regular doses of sedative as well."

"Good idea." We use the sedatives to keep smaller critters calm when we first put them in the rear pen and they're getting used to being around people. It'll help keep Star woolly-headed and chilled out, reducing her motive to wake up properly.

"But we're gonna have to pick up all the time we can on the highway," Uncle Z concludes. "It'll be close."

Close. Yeah. I was afraid he'd say that.

Saint Des, help? Don't let me have wrecked it all!

DARRYL

"Here!" I creep back into the workshop after a second foray to the house, holding a length of thick red cloth. "I'd better go feed the bottle'uns. I'll be back really soon."

I leave Mrs. Swayle transforming the fabric into something a bit bow-like and hurry to the young stock barn, mixing the milk as fast as I can. I drop the feeders into place quickly and take the final bottle in to the runty iggy. He's still fine, so I step quickly inside the safety ring as he grabs the teat and starts sucking. Yep, much healthier.

"How is he?"

I jump so hard I fumble the bottle and drop it. Behind my back, I press the talk button on my ScreamerBand. "Father Ben! You're up early!" I hear my voice come faintly from his band, but Dad and Harry will have heard it too. "Oh, oops!" I bring my hands back into sight as though I'd pressed the button accidentally, and bend to pick up the bottle. Did he hear anything from the workshop as he crossed the yard? Or did they hear the front door open? Or his footsteps? And stay quiet?

"I just wanted to check he was okay this morning and you didn't need any help."

"Oh, he's right as rain. You didn't need to get up." I realize how ungrateful I sound. "I mean, thanks for thinking about it. That was really nice of you. I'm just sorry you got up unnecessarily."

"Oh, I was getting up anyway." He smiles down at me and the iggy as it slurps the last few gulps from the bottle. "Well, I'll go and do morning prayer if all is well."

"I'm just coming, now."

I walk back to the barn door with him to be friendly, then watch him cross the yard. There are no signs of life from the workshop and he doesn't look that way. I guess he didn't hear anything suspicious. I dart along to the mix room to give everything a super-quick wash, then leave it draining and race back to the workshop.

"Father Ben's up! He came to check on the calf that was sick yesterday."

"We saw him go back to the house," says Dad. "We didn't realize until you warned us. I was just oiling the door hinges. Well done. Good thing we'd done all the noisy stuff. We were just waiting for you before wheeling it out."

Mrs. Swayle's red bow has been fastened over the finished van, so we ease the freshly-oiled workshop doors open and quietly push the van out into the yard, parking it facing the dining room window, where we'll eat breakfast.

Sighing and yawning, with many silent congratulatory fist bumps, the Christmas work party heads for their vehicles, all parked out of sight behind the barns. It's almost seven and the sky is lightening a lot now in anticipation of dawn. No sign of Father Benedict. Probably still in the guest room, praying.

Dad claps Harry and me on the shoulders. "Thanks, you two. You made the difference between it being finished or not, no question."

Harry swells with delight and I can't help beaming. Of course, the only bad thing about this is that it means Father Benedict can leave after lunch, as planned. But knowing him he'd have called a tow truck first thing to take his van to the city and get it repaired so he could get back to work—so it probably doesn't make any difference.

JOSHUA

"Umm, that smells good," I say, as I ease myself carefully down from the bedroom so I don't jolt my chest. I yawn, blinking like an owl. I didn't want to take pain pills since they make me woozy, though I'm sleepy enough anyway after just a few hours sleep.

"Aw, sit down, Josh. I got this."

I take my seat at the table that Uncle Z's managed to lower by resting it on Star's hip instead of its folding leg—it's *almost* level. We're awkwardly positioned at the end, on either side of Star's hind legs, in the only allosaur-free spaces large enough for chairs, but it's good enough.

"Leave that, Gold," I rescue my claw necklace from Gold's chewing. Normally we'd put on our newest clothes as well as our necklaces for something like Christmas, but today the necklace will have to do. We were both able to have a little wash, since we'd time to spare—a wash with a bowl of water won't chill Star, either. But we're not putting on our newest clothes to do a recovery—nor with these toothy chicks loose in here, neither. "*No*, Gold." I rumble allo-disapproval, making her draw back a bit. "Those are raptor claws. You should be scared of them at your age. Raptors would eat you up. Leave it."

Uncle Z removes the leg of lamb from—for a wonder—the oven part of the food processor instead of the frying pan and plunks it on the table. After adding bowls containing carrots and hash browns, he grabs the carving knife and sits down. Mostly we eat what we can hunt and forage for ourselves or buy direct from farms, but at Christmas we have some fancy city-bought stuff. In all honesty, it ain't really any tastier than the wild stuff, but novelty-value makes it a treat.

"Looks delish."

Uncle Z brushes this away and starts carving the lamb while I juggle allo-chicks. Gold's suddenly not interested in my claw necklace anymore!

"All right, that does it!" As once again he places a piece of meat on his plate only to have it snatched before he can dig in, Uncle Z leaps to his feet and grabs Gold by the scruff of the neck. "You uncivilized little louts are going in the critter cage until we've eaten!"

Watching him chasing them up and down the 'Vi as he tries to get all three of them in the cage at the same time makes me laugh so hard tears of pain ooze from my eyes.

"Gotcha!" He finally gets the door shut and shoots me a glare for my chortling.

"I woulda helped, honest," I tell him, "only you told me not to move my chest too much."

"Oh sure, 'cos laughing's so good for it." But he grins, seeing the funny side now the little menaces are secured, and we're finally free to enjoy our belated Christmas dinner.

DARRYL

"Father Ben?" I call up the stairs, once everything's on the table. "Breakfast's ready." I go back into the dining room and stand behind my seat. Dad and Harry are similarly positioned, not sitting yet because they want a good view of Father Benedict's reaction when he looks out the window. Harry's shifting from foot to foot in excitement, Dad's managing to stay still but his eyes gleam.

Trying not to dance around like Harry, I wait, as footsteps tread down the stairs.

"Morning," says Father Benedict.

"Morning, Father," we chorus.

"Can I trouble you to use the console after breakfast? I need to get myself a tow truck."

"Do you?" says Harry, though we'd agreed to wait until Father Benedict noticed the van for himself.

Father Benedict gives him a searching look. "Of course, Harry. Much as I'd like to spend the whole holiday period with you guys, there are a lot of people out there waiting for their Christmas Masses. Maybe I won't have to disappoint all of them."

"Maybe not any!" squeaks Harry, like he can't help himself. And starts shaking with suppressed laughter.

Father Benedict shoots a look at Dad, checking if he's worried about Harry's odd behavior. Dad looks back, straight-faced, so he glances at me. That means looking more towards the window and finally he glimpses the van outside. He does a double-take, then rushes to the window, staring at it.

"What... My van... Is it...?" His eyes run over the patches and fresh paint. Even the white clerical stripe has been refreshed. "Is it...*fixed?*"

"As fixed as we can make it," says Dad. "Road-worthy and habitable, that's for sure."

"But...but when did you...?"

"Half the local parishioners who are handy with repairs have been over here all night—along with Maurice and Tina," says Dad. "And Darryl and Harry helped too. Darryl did almost everything inside."

"Why, I...I..." Father Benedict blinks rapidly for a few moments, then makes a rush towards the door, as though to go and look more closely.

He halts suddenly, glancing at the table. "Ah, no, no, all this nice food is hot and ready. Let's eat. I'll go look afterwards, but...thank you. This is so unexpected! I thought a city-shop would be days over it, and I'd have to let so many people down. Thank you, all of you! I must thank all the others. I tell you what, I'll get Mrs. Grierson to make a rum bomb for every single person who helped! I'll collect them all next time I'm down that way."

Harry looks delighted—until Dad says, "That's a real nice idea for a thank you, Father Ben. But just one will do for the three of us."

Father Benedict shoots a glance at Harry, who's wilting in disappointment, and I'm pretty sure he winks, 'cos Harry brightens right up. I guess we'll be getting one bomb each!

I lick my lips. Fine by me!

JOSHUA

I stare out through the turret window, suppressing a yawn as I fight to stay at full alert. Uncle Z's down there checking things out, ready to set up the recovery, and

I'm his cover. I've gotta stay awake.

He's approaching the 'Vi again, shaking his head, his breath misting the early morning air. His voice comes over my earpiece. "Ain't nothing to fasten the cable to. And we can't fix a post into this frozen sludge."

"What do we do, then?" He don't sound despairing, just frustrated. There're usually options.

"I'm gonna go measure the distance to that outcrop of rock over there. We fasten every last cable together, it might reach."

He's soon heading off again, holding the laser measurer. I watch the screens on the turret console as I send the drone over to double-check behind the outcrop. All clear. He reaches the outcrop quick enough, stands beside it and points the laser back to the 'Vi, taking the reading—then whistles. "'Kay, we're on. Just. We'll have to set a ring into the rock; it won't reach around the back."

Darn. That's an extra hour's work. Still, the news is more a relief than anything. The lighter it got, the worse things looked. No trees, no boulders, no solid ground anywhere near. A very bad place to be bogged. Bad enough even without Star onboard, since the longer we stay the more firmly we'll be frozen in. But drilling a ring into the rock is possible and nothing but work. We can deal with that.

I certainly can't accuse Uncle Z of wasting time. Ten minutes later he's back at the boulder, starting drilling. I watch the surrounding landscape as he works, my eyes moving from horizon to middle ground to near ground to screens, regularly circling the area with the drone to see behind the few obstacles and sending it further out to check for more distant threats.

It's very quiet, though. Those critters that haven't migrated south are still nestled in their burrows and sheltered sleeping spots, waiting for the warmer part of the day before emerging to hunt for food. Hopefully we'll be done by then.

It ain't getting light properly, though. I mean it's daylight enough to work, but there's a grey smothered hue to everything. A hint of purple in the air... I turn and scan the northern sky, and now I'm looking for it my eyes pick out a faint, ominous deep purple line on the horizon. "Uncle Z, I think there's a killer-chiller building up north."

He swings around, straightening, and peers that way too.

"Outage." He turns back to the outcrop and goes back to work without saying anything else. He don't need to say anything. The polar vortex storms that ravage the rural areas of this state in winter and make it virtually uninhabitable are unpleasant enough at the best of times—and terrifying. The way the temperature plummets—like some massive frost demon is inhaling and sucking every scrap of warmth from the world—has to be experienced to be believed—which is why there are always plenty of frozen bodies to recover every spring, mostly city-folk.

The high winds and blizzards are a minor inconvenience in comparison. But the storm will freeze everything diamond-hard, and, at this time of year, depending on the subsequent weather, it could take days, weeks, or even a couple of months for the wetland—and the snow the storm will pile over us—to thaw enough for us to get loose. If we can't get out of here before the storm hits we'll probably die—or almost worse, should we get a satellite lock-on in time, we'll have to call for help. Getting rescued by Highway Patrol is the ultimate humiliation for any hunter.

Not that Highway Patrol would be very interested in our current predicament—they're *Highway* Patrol, not wilderness patrol. If you ain't fairly close to a highway or road of some kind, you're expected to rescue yourself. If you're a hunter, anyway, but who else would be out here? Expendable, that's how city-folk see us. A city-person stuck out here, well, they'd probably send a big shiny chopper, if the weather allowed. Us? If we were lucky, they might dispatch a patroller to the closest 'Vi-park to let the guys know we were stuck. And someone would come, almost certain, but in a scenario like this, they'd probably be too late.

Uncle Z's movements, already quick and deliberate, have sped up even more. He gets the ring fixed in place in forty minutes. Go, Uncle Z!

"Okay." Uncle Z is heading back to the 'Vi, lugging the drill. "I've just got to run the cable out. We're nearly ready."

He doesn't drag the heavy recovery cable out there, of course, he just takes a thick spiderline, runs it through the ring and brings it back to the winch, using that to tow the cable out. Then he stakes down the end of the cable to stop it springing and coiling, and unfastens it from the drum. Disconnects the empty drum and removes it from the spindle. Fetches the cable drum from the nearside winch and heaves it into place, then attaches one cable to the other. Operates the winch again until that drum is empty. Then repeats the process with rear drum and offside drum. Adds the small length of back-up cable from the exterior locker. And that's the lot.

I wait anxiously as he trots off towards the boulder again. Has it reached? If it hasn't...

Something catches my eye on the horizon. I swing my rifle up and look through my telescopic sights. A cluster of small specks. Outage!

"Uncle Z, get inside. Piranha'saurs."

"Aw, heck. How close? Have I got a minute?"

I estimate the distance. "Depends how fast you can run over this terrain and how many of them you want to get a taste of you. You're out of the scatter gun's range over there, so unless you want me to try and pick them off one by one with a .22..."

Uncle Z swears, but in the circumstances I'm not surprised when he dashes the rest of the way to the boulder instead of returning. He grabs the end of the tow cable and hauls it...to the ring? Yes! As he readies the shackle, I grab the piranha'saur scatter gun from under the console and raise the windows on that side of the turret, then check the position of the shoal. "C'mon, Uncle Z! They're coming!"

The inquisitive little biters are definitely coming to check us out. Uncle Z's wearing ScentBlock cream but he's moving around, and there's no way to stop the 'Vi looking interesting.

I hear a clink through my earpiece. "Okay, it's done. I'm on my way."

He sprints for the 'Vi. I check the shoal again. It's gonna be close. They've seen him and they're coming full speed, now, their tiny shapes a blur of motion as they race over the snow. I don't urge Uncle Z to hurry again—if he slips and falls he'll lose even more time. Ignoring my twinging rib, I raise the gun to my shoulder and wait for them to come within range.

Uncle Z's about thirty feet away. The critters are

fifty feet from him, closing fast. But...in range. I fire twice—*ouch*, this gun always kicks like some ancient cannon—and half the frontrunners fall. The rest hesitate, milling uncertainly. This is a wild area; they may never have been hunted.

Their delay has cost them any chance of a taste of Uncle Z. He's reached the 'Vi, and he's getting in. The door hisses shut.

He climbs up to the turret and stands slapping his hands together to warm them. "Pah, I thought I was gonna get nipped, then. Get bitten in here, get bitten out there. What a Christmas."

Our own three little nippers are still safely in the critter cage, so they can't slip out any time Uncle Z opens the door. Speaking of open things...I quickly close the windows against the cold, shooting another glance at the northern sky. Not much change, yet.

"Well, get down to the driver's seat, and let's see if we can get out of here." Uncle Z moves to the turret winch control.

Carefully, I ease my way down the ladder, the pain from my chest making me breathe hard. I scramble over Star's tail and settle into the driver's seat as gently as possible. Once I have the engine running, Uncle Z very slowly starts the winch moving. The cable twangs as the slack is taken up, then the 'Vi jolts slightly as it tightens. The ice around us creaks and shudders. But doesn't break.

"Careful!" The words are out before I can stop them. If we snap that cable, we're in really big trouble.

All I get through my earpiece is a tolerant silence, but Uncle Z only runs the winch a little harder before easing it off again. "Well, we tried simple," he says. "We're gonna have to crack the ice loose around us. And if that don't work, we'll have to haul that two and a half ton allo out of here double-quick."

I wince as I climb back up to the turret, and not just in pain. If we have to put Star out there our chances of keeping the piranha'saurs off her for long are slim and even if we did she'd freeze to death in the storm. And there's not much chance we could haul her back in without bogging ourselves again immediately. No, if she has to come out, she's not coming back in. Lightening the load that way really is a last resort. "We could take other stuff out first."

"We ain't got nothing that adds up to her weight. That's the only reason we went through the ice in the first place. There's a good chance we can just break ourselves free, anyway. It's getting colder. The storm's gonna help us—if we time it right."

I glance again at the purple clouds on the horizon. Yeah. So long as we can get out before the temperature drops so far the ice re-freezes faster than we can break it, the frozen marsh will hold us better than it did last night.

"Okay," Uncle Z adds. "I'll suit up and start hacking. Keep 'em at bay as much as you can."

"I will."

I watch guiltily as Uncle Z soon emerges again, now wearing a heavy leather tunic for extra protection from the shoal and carrying an axe. I got us into this, but 'cos of my rib, I won't be doing any of the hard physical work.

No time to worry about it, now. I raise the scatter gun and let drive at the shoal again as they flow towards Uncle Z. They peel off and fall back, so I hold my fire as Uncle Z begins hacking at the ice to the side of the bogged front. He'll work all the way around the 'Vi, leaving the very front almost untouched so there's plenty of solid ice for the 'Vi to come up onto.

It's all more time, though. Even if we out-run the storm, what chance the tranquilizers will last, now?

DARRYL

Father Benedict seems lost for words as he peers inside his van. We snuck his gift bedding and quilt from the family room where we gave out the gifts and put it on his bed, so it all looks very homey and normal.

"I really...I don't know what to say. This was so kind of you all. Your whole Christmas night, all of you...

Even Maurice and Tina…I can't thank you enough."

"A rum bomb will be more than enough," mutters Harry, licking his lips and making Father Benedict laugh.

"We didn't do it for the thanks, Father Ben," I say. "We just wanted to fix your little home for you."

"Well, thank you, anyway. I'm sorry I have to leave right after lunch. I've a Mass to the east of here tonight, and another tomorrow right up north. You know what Christmas week is like for rural clergy. Trying to be everywhere at once. And now I will be, after all—well, as much as I ever can! Thanks to all of you."

We all shrug and get a little hot in the face and mutter "don't mention it" some more until finally he climbs up into the van for a closer look and stops embarrassing us.

JOSHUA

"Okay." Rubbing his hands and stamping his feet to get warm, Uncle Z goes to the winch control again. "Let's do this."

"I've said five chaplets to Saint Des while you were hacking," I tell him, wanting him to know I've been doing all I can.

"Good. Let's see if he's listening."

Yeah. I head down the ladder again. Surely he is,

though? I mean, he don't want Star put out in the cold to be et, right? Guess it's not up to him, though. He's only a saint, not God. Dad always made a point about that when other hunters talked like they'd forgot.

Uncle Z starts the winch again once I've got the engine running. *Shudder.* Cable's taut. Not much sound of ice, now, 'cos it's all loose already, though it'll freeze up again fast enough in this temperature. Grinding and creaking from the front. Cracking. The ice is breaking as the winch pulls the 'Vi into it. Hopefully it'll build up until the wheels can get a grip on it and haul us out... *Come on...*

Saint Des?

Yep, we are moving. Very slowly. I can see the ice bunching up in front of us. Some is getting driven down, under the wheels. Good. More shuddering. Selecting the very lowest combination of gears, very gently I press the gas pedal. A lurch. Are the wheels gripping something?

"I think we've got some traction."

"Take it slow," Uncle Z says from my earpiece.

"Yep." I keep the revs low, just enough to keep the wheels biting and take some strain off the cable. If I apply excessive force and the ice crumples it won't help.

We're coming out. We are. Inch by inch we're creeping up, the vehicle coming back onto an even keel as the front wheels emerge. We're not out of the woods yet. The rear wheels have to go into the same pit. But the front wheels will drag them out more easily than the back ones could push our front out. And we've still got the winch cable helping.

Yep. In it goes. *Jolt, shudder, thud.* Out of the corner of my eye, I see Star's tail twitch. *Outage!* No time to think about it now. We can't stop yet.

Slowly, the rear wheels come out again. I drive steadily forwards until the first winch cable is all wound up, then I have to stop. Up to the turret again—*ow*—while Uncle Z jumps out to change the winch drum. The piranha'saurs are still there, watching, but they're getting smarter, and I don't have to shoot any this time, which my chest is especially glad of. Uncle Z drives this time, while I operate the winch, to save me going up and down extra times.

Once all the cables are wound, we head straight on to firm ground. Only once we've all four wheels on rock do I say, "Star needs tranquing again ASAP. I saw her move."

"So did I, just now. Come down and make us a hot drink and a sandwich while I deal with her."

I obey. But despite the need to hurry, Uncle Z spends a long time staring at the syringe and bottle and muttering to himself as he calculates. The amount he injects her with is far less than before. We're gonna have to do it far more often and even so, things could get a little...interesting.

You got this, Saint Des.

DARRYL

"I'm going to call him Lion," says Harry, coming out to wave Father Benedict off with the cage in his hand. "Lions aren't afraid of farmcats."

I don't say anything. Nor does Dad. From his expression, he's also trying to decide whether "Lion" will live longer if he's more afraid of Psycho Cat, or less.

Father Benedict just smiles. "Well, that's a strong name. Would you like me to give him a pet blessing before I go?"

"Yeah!"

Lion gets his pet blessing, my rifle gets its tool blessing, and Father Benedict gives his van a vehicle blessing. "Since it's been kind of resurrected," he says. "Almost feels like having a new one."

Dad pops back into the house in response to a ping from our ScreamerBands—a weather alert has arrived—and comes back out shaking his head.

"What's coming?" I ask.

"They've just issued a storm warning for Exception and Yoming. The lightning-freeze they were hoping might not happen up in Tana State is building and it looks like the tail will hit us quite hard."

"*Great*. When's it going to reach us?"

"Tomorrow morning, most likely." Dad turns to Father Benedict. "Did you say you're going north? Maybe you should stay here another day, after all."

"East, today. North tomorrow. I can wait until the storm blows through tomorrow before travelling on. The heater's working, right?"

"I tested it myself." Immediately, I'm gripped with a stupid worry whether I really checked it carefully enough. If he mis-times his journey, his life could depend on that heater. But I did. I know I did.

Even so, I'm not offended when he climbs into the van and switches the heater on, moving it through its settings, before turning it off again. Some things you've just got to check yourself.

"I'm not surprised no one farms in Tana any more—at least, not in the winter," says Harry. "The tails of those storms are awful enough."

"It's a bad week for one," says Father Benedict, looking grim. "So many people travelling between cities to see their folks."

"They close the highways up there," says Dad. "It's only idiots who try to sneak down the back roads who get caught in those things. And hunters. But hunters don't die in them."

"Don't *often* die in them," corrects Father Benedict, still looking glum. "I said several Requiem Masses for guys who'd died in those killer storms, when I was a city priest ministering to the 'Vi-park. All it takes is an equipment malfunction or a crash or something unforeseen."

"But *this* week," I point out, hoping to cheer him up, "there *won't* be any hunters out and about, will there? They'll all be in their camps or wherever they have their base, with their families. Won't be anyone out there at all. So maybe it's a good week for one, after all."

Father Benedict smiles at last. "Maybe you're right. Well, I've a full tank of fuel and a heater, and I won't shift tomorrow until it's safe. I'd better be going."

Regretfully—and a little uneasily after the storm news—we say goodbye and watch him drive away. It's a dangerous life for a rural priest; long, long hours on the road. Sometimes I think they should get HabVis, not mere vans, even with a priest hole for emergencies. But then the diocese couldn't even afford to send out as many rural priests as it does now.

Guess SOS vans will have to do.

JOSHUA

Since Uncle Z's done all the heavy work this morning and I did get a few hours sleep, he goes for a nap while I take the wheel again. It's snowing heavily, now, the wind whipping the flakes sideways, and I keep the headlights on even though it's early afternoon. I fasten the roll harness too, though it hurts my chest, 'cos these ain't exactly optimum conditions and I've had a good reminder earlier why Dad and Uncle Z always thought it so important. Sure, I've got a cracked rib, but it's better than smashing my head on the windshield.

Even with the heaters on the cold is growing intense, though we're hours yet from the "devil's inhale." I can smell the gathering storm in the air, though I'd be hard pressed to describe the scent.

I've already slipped into my outdoor jacket and mittens and drawn a blanket over my legs. I've thrown several over Star's huge, emaciated form, along with a couple of spare sleeping bags, though we'll want the sleeping bags back, before this is over. I've put yet another blanket down under the cab's hot air vent, passenger-side, for the chicks, though Gold prefers my lap still, creeping under my blanket and almost knocking if off every time she wriggles.

"Argh, go to sleep, Gold!" I make another grab for the blanket as she shifts, and try to tuck it in behind me to make it stay, growling at her disapprovingly.

I drive as fast as I can in the snow, desperate not to lose any more time and to stay ahead of the storm if possible. We won't be able to keep going through the eye if it catches up with us, no way. We'll have to stop and hunker down and wait for it to blow over—more time lost. The only good thing about a killer-chiller is they do go over quick. Some people call them lightning-freezes, in fact.

The visibility's getting worse and worse, and the temperature's dropping. I'd guess outrunning the thing is no longer an option but I'm determined to keep us moving. Uncle Z's sleeping soundly so I can just keep going as long as possible.

By late afternoon the chicks are shivering under the hot air vent, blanket or no blanket. I ease the 'Vi gently to a halt, hoping to avoid waking Uncle Z. When he sees how bad it is he'll probably want to stop immediately and prepare to wait it out. But every wasted minute just increases the chances we'll have to shoot Star before this is over.

Quickly, I empty Uncle Z's clothes' drawers, laying shirts and pants and anything and everything over Star to replace the sleeping bags, which I put back as the top layer, easy to remove when we want them. I cut the end off some socks and pull them up onto her forearms, making a double layer. A pair of Uncle Z's old winter mittens go over her three-clawed hands. A couple of thermal socks and a fur-lined rubber boot onto the tip of her tail, another frostbite weak spot. Her stocky hind legs and feet I bundle up in scarves and t-shirts.

In the wild, whether she survived would depend on

how healthy she was and how good a shelter she found to huddle in. Starved as she is, she'd die for sure out there, and she's in danger even in here. The main living area ain't meant to stay warm in those sorts of temperatures. I've done what I can for her, anyway. What to do about the chicks, though?

Two fleece hats provide part of the answer. Both Uncle Z's, but I can't get to my stuff with him asleep up there. I know he's already wearing his best one, so I quickly cut little holes for neck, forearms, and legs, and wrestle Frankie and Myrrh into the makeshift jackets, my reassuring croons not having much effect. They roll on the floor when released, biting and tugging at the material, but they're so cold and miserable by now they quickly creep back to their nest under the vent and curl up again. I flip the blanket over them for a bit of extra protection.

I don't have a third hat down here, though. Gold's been following me around, peeping pitifully, shivering, asking to go back in my lap. I reckon her fondness for my warm lap is one of the reasons why she's got so tame so quick—if she nipped me, I'd push her off and not let her back on for a while, so she's stopped doing it.

When I pick her up, her skin feels cool under her feathers. She's too small to deal with these temperatures without help.

"Well," I tell her, "you do seem to have got the hang

of the 'no biting' thing quite well. And I don't know what else to do with you." Unzipping my parka a little way, I take my life—or at least my nipples—in my hand and tuck her inside, crooning softly in reassurance. Zipping it up, I wait to find out her opinion of this new berth.

Approval. At least, she curls up in the warm with every sign of contentment—which is to say, without any painful objections.

"Good girl," I murmur, settling into the driver's seat again. Star's as warm as I can make her without waking Uncle Z and so are the chicks. I'll try and put some more miles behind us. I glance in the rearview screen. The entire sky behind is purple-black, now, a massive wall of angry bruised clouds bearing down on us.

With a shudder, I press the gas again.

DARRYL

This Christmas isn't improving. Thanks to the incoming lightning-freeze we've spent the afternoon inspecting and securing everything on the farm, making sure windows are closed, checking heaters, draining down any water system that won't withstand the cold, and a hundred other things. No time to zero my new rifle. No time for Harry to start training Lion. No time for any Christmas fun. Or even to take a nap...

But it's all done by dusk. Nothing left to do tomorrow other than turn on barn heaters, check they're running properly, and drive around the 'saur stock to make sure they've all gathered in the storm shelters. Pre-storm is always kinda stressful. I know what Harry means. Even getting lashed by the tail of the thing as it's well on the way to blowing itself out is horrible. Exception's got a really nice climate, in general. Fairly mild winters, not too hot summers. But every now and then, nature hammers us with ice and fury. Guess it keeps us grateful for the rest.

It's all done, anyway, and finally we can go inside and relax and remember that it's actually Christmas. Yeah, I'm feeling kinda grumpy again. Usually we'd have a special Eastern European meal tonight, to celebrate Saint Stephen's Day, but I'm too tired to even contemplate starting on it. We can have the last of the Christmas Day leftovers. Dad—who didn't even get the couple of hours' sleep I got—obviously feels the same, because he nods straight off in his armchair without even mentioning the meal.

Since I can't do much with my rifle now it's dark, I dip into my new book, but I keep yawning and eventually I put it aside to watch Harry making a very premature attempt to handle Lion. After laughing a little harder than he appreciates, I make it up to him by fetching a bandage for his finger, after which he sends Lion for quiet time by hooding his cage again and picks up his new prayer book.

Soon he recites:

"From T. rex' jaws
From raptor's claws,
From life indoors,
From all our flaws,
Deliver us, Lord.
And smile upon us,
Mother mild."

Dad—who woke up when Harry yelped—snorts. "That's the Our Father bead prayer from the Chaplet of Saint Desmond. If you tell me you're only just learning that, Darryl and I will have to disown you."

Harry sniffs. "Of course I know it! But it's my favorite, and it's right here on page one. Do you know the centerpiece prayer, though?"

Dad looks suddenly sheepish. "Uh, I know bits of it. Most people skip it, though."

"Not hunters, according to this! They always include it. It's like, heavy. Listen! O Lord, you know of what we are made, dust and clay..."

JOSHUA

"...Our days are like grass,

We bloom like a flower in the meadow;

The wind blows and we are gone.

If you take our breath, we return to earth,

And our plans this day come to nothing."

As I breathe in, the cold chills my throat even with the heaters running on full. I peer through the windshield, gripping the wheel tightly as I struggle to see. Visibility's down to a few feet and we're crawling. But the terrain's safe, so we're still moving.

I've been awake for a ridiculously long time, now, with only those couple of hours sleep this morning, but I don't feel sleepy. Exhausted, but not sleepy. I can feel the devil's inhale building behind us. Not yet, but it's coming. Hard to believe it's gonna get even colder than this. But I do, 'cos I've been through it before. It's gonna get a lot colder. I'm praying as I drive, one chaplet after another, fighting the rising sense of dread these storms induce in their victims.

"You know my resting and my rising,

Marking when I work or lie down,

All my ways are naked before you.

If I assume feathers at dawn and soar to the heavens,

You are there.

If I lie in the grave, you are there.

Your right hand grips me forever."

I jump almost out of my skin as a hand grips my shoulder, barely choking back a yell. Gold turns over sleepily inside my jacket and settles again. "Uncle Z! Heck, did you time that deliberately?" I ease us to a halt. I can't talk and drive in these conditions.

His grin is brief and strained. He stares at the snow lashing the windshield. "We should stop, Josh."

"We can't stop until we absolutely have to! You know we're running out of tranqs. We can still see, so we can still drive."

Uncle Z glances at the view ahead. "I guess we have different notions of what 'see' means, but in theory." He shoots a look back into the living area. "Is there any item of clothing I possess the allo *ain't* wearing?"

I think for a moment, then point under the vent, where Frankie and Myrrh are curled up together, shivering in their little hat-coats, having pushed their blanket off again.

Uncle Z looks like he can't decide whether to laugh or swear. "Right." He eyes me. "You'd better get some rest. You look done-in."

"'Kay, but you're gonna keep going, right?"

Uncle Z glances out at the blizzard yet again. "For a little longer, I guess. Ain't promising more than that. Bed. Now."

I obey, struggling over Star's tail on rubbery legs.

I'm even more tired than I realized. I use the head and down a mug of plain hot water for heat and hydration, then drag myself straight up into my berth. I'm not even *thinking* about washing in this temperature.

Only as I'm settling into my sleeping bag and zipping myself in do I remember I've still got Gold inside my jacket. Ah, what the heck, I'm wearing gloves and if she nibbles my nose I'll wake up fast enough. I reckon she's just gonna hunker there in the warm, anyway. She ain't dumb, for an allo.

DARRYL

A ping sounds from my ScreamerBand just as I'm heading up the stairs to bed—rather early, but I can't keep my eyes open. Another weather update. I pause and wait while Dad comes out into the hall and bends over the House Control.

"Any change?" I ask.

"It'll be here early tomorrow, sometime after eight o'clock. We're going to have to get moving fast tomorrow—it looks like a bad one."

"Shall I feed the calves early?" Oh, great. This Christmas really does keep improving.

"I think you'd better. I'll drive the fence early, too. We should be ready to do the pre-storm jobs by six-thirty at the latest."

"Okay. Uh, good night."

"Night, Darryl."

I head upstairs, shivering, though it's not that cold yet. There's something about these storms that—how did it put it in that old adventure story?—chills the marrow. Thank God the storm didn't come on Christmas Eve. There's no way we could've got to Father Benedict in a lightning-freeze. Heater or not, most likely we'd have found him afterwards, lying there in his priest hole, frozen, like one of those holy statues in a medieval cathedral.

I shudder and push the thought away. It didn't happen. And it won't happen tonight because there'll be no one out there, right?

But just in case any silly city-folk have been that determined to reach their relatives in another city just as planned—or in case there *are* any hunters out there, braving the storm's onslaught in the fragile safety of their HabVi—I kneel down and pray a decade of the rosary for those in peril from the storm. And only then go to bed.

Feeling a little less grumpy.

JOSHUA

"Make some room, Josh." Uncle Z's voice. He's patting my feet, shouting to be heard over the howling wind.

"The eye of the storm's almost on us. Visibility zero. We need to hunker."

Sleepily, I poke my head out of my sleeping bag, drawing my legs up to clear the doorway, then sit up and move so I can start taking things from him. Briskly, he passes up several thermos flasks, a few food items, and a large number of water bottles, which I stack against the rear wall. It looks an excessive amount of liquid for a storm that'll pass over in a few hours but he'll have dumped all our freshwater and wastewater by now—our tank insulation can't withstand what's coming—so we'll have to make do with liquids in the fridge and freezer and what we have here until we find a stream. A running stream. Or we'll be boiling snow on the stovetop. Not for the first time.

He slides his rifle in, then, to my surprise—and relief—he pops Frankie and Myrrh up into the bedroom. Well, that saves an argument!

I must be smirking slightly, 'cos he shrugs. "They're gonna freeze down there, plain fact." He's peering around the berth. "Yeah, I couldn't find the third one. I figured it was up here, but—"

"She's inside my jacket. I only had two hats."

"You mean, *I* only had two hats." Uncle Z rolls his eyes, but his good hat's on his head still, and I know he's not really mad. "You sure do like to live dangerously."

"She's the tamest. Been good so far. How's Star? Is she gonna be okay?"

Uncle Z shrugs. "Shutters are closed, I've left the heater vent open to the living area"—he winces; we'd never normally try to heat the entire cab and living area throughout a killer-chiller—"she'll live or she won't, ain't nothing more we can do—we need these." He tosses the spare sleeping bags up.

"Uh, *yeah*, there is!" I pull the nearest drawer open, tossing a handful of shirts to Uncle Z. "Put my clothes on her instead."

"At this rate, we might need them ourselves," mutters Uncle Z, but he must be worried too because he climbs down again and keeps arranging the clothes over Star until I've passed them all out. "I jabbed her again," he adds, once he's climbed back up and shut the door. "We're gonna have to stretch the tranqs even further now, so I added another big dose of sedative."

He's shivering as he slides one of the spare sleeping bags over his normal one and puts the other over the foot of my bag, leaving me to wriggle it up. Even with the heater on, it's cold, now. I shift over so he can scramble straight into his doubled sleeping bag. The berth is only seven foot by four and four foot high, so it's a bit of a squeeze. But the smaller space the better, just now. The warmer, anyway.

The wind is so loud Frankie and Myrrh cower,

tummies pressed to the mattress, their little eyes flicking around as they try to figure out what's going on. I can't even talk allo to them, in this racket—they wouldn't hear. Inside my jacket, Gold seems calmer.

Uncle Z nods to the flasks. "Soup, coffee, hot chocolate. Chocolate and nuts. We're set. This won't last long. Never does. Let's have a bowl of soup and tuck ourselves in quick, before the devil inhales."

I'm ravenous—when I check the clock I find I've been asleep the better part of two hours—and I eagerly down two cups of soup with some bread, and a mug of hot chocolate to follow. It's all drinking temperature the moment it's poured. Even with the heater. Without it, we'd be lucky to survive the storm.

In normal storms we can use the main engine as a back-up heater—though we'd have to decamp to the cab and huddle by the vent and it's a toss-up whether we'd lose more heat in that far less insulated space than we'd gain—but if the main heater shut down during the devil's inhale we might be overcome by the cold before we could reach it and it wouldn't be warm enough, anyway. No prizes for guessing why we strip down the main heater and service it every fall, without fail.

The main heater has a storm setting so it will prioritize keeping the bedroom warm—handy in a lesser storm when we can leave the vent open to the living area and it will just warm it a little to keep things from freezing—but for a storm like this we'd normally divert every scrap of heat to where we are. How much heat will the storm setting actually allow Star through the worst of it? Still, she's better off than she'd be outside.

Once we've had our fill and most of the flasks have been stowed inside the foot end of our sleeping bags to keep warmer, Uncle Z unscrews one last flask. "This one's meat broth. For the chicks."

"Ah, good." I breathe out in relief. "I was just thinking I'd better go down and get them something."

"I bet you would've, too. Well, no, 'cos I wouldn't let you. Too late for that." Uncle Z pours a mug while I fish Gold from my jacket. "Here, feed them. Be quick. I'll get the storm blanket fixed."

I hold onto the mug to prevent it going everywhere and, after momentary hesitance because of the food's unfamiliar heat, Gold is soon dipping her head and gulping the broth down, snapping at Frankie and Myrrh as they sneak mouthfuls. Fortunately my heavily gloved hands look far less appetizing than the broth so even the thwarted pair pay them little attention.

Once Gold's sated she runs straight to my lap and scrabbles at my jacket, so I pull the zip down a little way and in she goes, her feathery tail swiping over my cheek. Hastily, one-handed, I fasten my coat again. The devil's due to inhale, all right. We need to hurry.

Uncle Z has pulled the thin, super-warm storm blanket from the emergency cupboard and spread it over the two of us, zipping it around the bottom of the wall almost to the top of the berth, ready to be pulled up over our heads. "Come on, tuck yourself in," he urges. "There's no time."

Frankie and Myrrh have eaten their fill, but they're shivering hard as the temperature plunges—and the worst is still to come. "Oh, in you go, then." I scoop them up in my gloved hands and tuck them inside my sleeping bag. Not inside my coat. They'd barely fit, and even if Gold was willing to share—unlikely—I don't trust them that much.

Awkwardly, with three sharp-toothed chicks to shift around and an unhappy rib, I wriggle deep down into my sleeping bag, zip it right up over my head and put my back to Uncle Z. It's not only the easiest way to fit into the small space, it also allows us to pool body heat. This all sure used to be a squeeze with Dad too. Warmer, though.

Outside, the wind howls like a million lost souls bound for hell.

Heck, I wish Dad were here. He used to put his arm around me and hold me tight. I guess I'm a bit old for that, but nobody feels very grown-up when they're lying in the devil's mouth, waiting.

I feel Uncle Z chuck the blanket over us, zipping it

up around the top of the berth. The storm strips around the bottom of the wall provide dim light, some of which makes it into my sleeping bag. The heater vent is at the bottom of the wall, too, and we've just reduced the area it's warming—trying to warm—to about a quarter. If the heater dies on us, the hi-tech blanket is supposed to give us a chance of survival, too, but I wouldn't pin high hopes on it.

"Right," bellows Uncle Z over the wind, sliding well down into his own sleeping bag, zipping it up over his head and rolling to put his back solidly against mine. "Let's say a chaplet and try to sleep through this darn thing."

Dad was always the one to initiate family prayers, Uncle Z more often prays in private, so it only confirms what I already know, that these storms are real dangerous. I bet he's brought his mom's—my Grandma I never met—rosary up here with him, the special one that always hangs over our photo frame along with Momma Matriarch's blue feather.

I yell back, "Sounds good."

I guess we're both scared, but we won't mention it, because what's the point? We'll live or we'll die, but there ain't nothing more we can do now—except this.

"In the name of the Father, the Son, and the Holy Spirit..."

With a suddenness that makes me start even though

I've been waiting for it with nerves tight, the wind's howl shatters into absolute silence. Silence so pure you could be floating around in space. We both instinctively stop speaking as the ghostly hush envelops everything.

Then the little noises start. *Ting. Ping. Creak. Ping. Ting.* Everything in the 'Vi is contracting as the extreme cold of the storm's eye whips away any remaining heat. My breath mists in front of my face, despite the heater's efforts. I grab the top of my sleeping bag in my gloved hand and fold it under, padding the crack with the scarf I have ready, before laying my head on it to pin it down, sealing myself in completely.

I can feel Uncle Z wriggling, doing the same. I don't really want to sleep—if the heater shuts off I want to know so I can look death in the face, the way Dad did, rather than just slide off into the darkness without ever waking—but I'm so tired I know I will. When he finishes getting comfy and jumps straight to the centerpiece prayer, voice muffled, I join right in.

"O Lord, you know of what we are made,

dust and clay..."

4

FEAST OF THE HOLY FAMILY

DARRYL

The howling of the wind finally snatches me fully awake. What a racket! Climbing out of bed, I wrap my quilt around myself against the cold and go to the window, then raise the shutters slightly. Snow hammers the glass immediately. Nasty. Hard to believe they'll have had it far, far worse up north.

My clock says five AM. My alarm is set for half past and I don't think I'll sleep again. Might as well get moving. *This Christmas really—* I manage to choke off the end of that thought. Since when am I such a whiner? I was just so looking forward to some Christmas downtime and it really isn't happening. Before we know it Dad will be chivying us to get back to our TuteApps and Christmas will be over.

I've almost finished dressing—lots of thermals—when there's a tap on the door. "Ryl, are you up? Storm's moving faster than predicted; it's big and bad, we need to bustle."

"I'm just coming, Dad."

When I get down to the hall he's there pulling on warm outer layers. "I'm going to drive the fence, you feed the calves quick, then we can go around the stock together. Harry's just getting up. He's going to do the heaters."

"Okay." Dad would never leave the safety of our inner fence on his own, in this weather, so I was expecting to go with him. I pull on my own layers quickly, then put my rifle over my shoulder so I don't have to come back to the house for it.

"Ready?"

"Yep." *Saint Des, watch over us...*

Dad opens the door and the gale bursts into the hall in an explosion of snow. I follow Dad out quickly and he shuts the door again.

The cold steals my breath, searing my throat, and I pull my balaclava up over my mouth, pressing my hand over the top, even as I brace myself against the driving wind.

"I'll pick you up from the barn," Dad yells in my ear.

I nod and bolt across the yard, one hand over my

face, the other clutching my hood. The wind buffets me, making me weave as I try to force my way against it. Snow lashes into my eyes, blinding me. Finally my hands touch the slick no-climb metal of the barn wall. Bending forward, I plow my way into the teeth of the gale until I reach the door.

The relief as that door closes behind me, shutting out the storm... The wind still howls around the barn, but inside is sanctuary. I mix the milk quickly and dart around, dropping the feeders into place without petting even Janey. The calves, whether bovine or 'saur, all shift and stamp uneasily, letting go of the teats regularly to look around and roll their eyes at the strangeness in the air. I rinse everything quickly, get my gloves back on, and am waiting behind the door when Dad pulls up and honks.

A chilly, breath-stealing rush and I'm in the truck, teeth chattering.

"Heck, how do people survive these things up north, Dad? They're, like, five times worse, right?"

Dad shrugs as he pulls away. "Well, Father Ben was right. People out in them often don't. People in normal cars, never. Nothing but summer farming up there, now. Anyway, we're down here, thank God. Harry's in the barns, turning the heaters on. Lord willing we can be around the stock nice and quick and get back in the house well before the eye arrives."

"Amen," I say fervently.

Dad has to drive really slowly, though, because we can't see very far ahead. Once through the main gates we head across the first pasture towards the storm shelter, out near the outer fence. Some pastures are very odd shapes due to the need to include one, because most are a large outcrop or hillock, the south side cut flat so the stock can get up against it for better protection from the lightning-freezes that always come from the north. Making artificial ones is a heap of work. But no farmer has a fraction of the barn space to house all their 'saur-stock through a storm — not unless they're farming small delicacy breeds.

The iggies in this pasture are all gathered in the shelter — we can't see most of them for howling snow but the handheld thermal scanner allows me to perform a head-count — so we drive under the wide-spaced, two-strand dividing fence.

The edmos next door have got themselves to safety too. But as we enter the next pasture my pass with the scanner pauses. "Bear left, Dad. There's a juvenile."

A male, we discover, as we get close enough to see it. Biting off grass and swallowing as though oblivious to the storm. We circle it, honking, even nudging its front legs with our rubber bumper until we finally get it moving in the right direction.

"Go on, you dim-witted beast," says Dad, as we

herd it along. "Thank God you don't look like a possible stud-animal. You have *got* to go."

"He's not kill-weight yet, Dad."

"No," says Dad darkly, "but when he is..."

I laugh. Ah-ha, there's the rest of Mr. Not-enough-survival-instinct-to-fill-a-teaspoon's herd. Dad drives in a big semi-circle around them, so I can get a count. "That's all of them," I confirm.

"Good."

We get through the next pastures without any hitch, a full headcount in each. "Second to last one," I say happily, as we pass under another fence.

But once Dad's circled the shelter I have to say, "Go around again. I'm missing some."

Second time, my count goes up by one mare, but... "There's one mare and all five of her last season calves missing." I swing the scanner over the pasture, searching, though it's so cold now it's reducing the effective distance considerably. "There might be something over there..." I point.

Dad heads that way as fast as he dares and soon four of the missing calves pass us, up on their hind legs, running towards the shelter, though they keep pausing to look anxiously over their shoulders.

"Looks like the mother's sent them on to shelter." I say. "Yep, the mother's up ahead," I say, as we get closer. "Running back and forth like she wants to go to the shelter but she doesn't want to at the same time. But I can't see the last calf."

But we can with our eyes, as we finally get close enough to make out the mare. A still form lies in the snow, a light dusting already coating it, except where the mother's pushed it off, nudging the calf to try to get it up.

There's no heat signature.

JOSHUA

I'm hot. The awareness gradually breaks in on my slumber. Very hot. I open my eyes. The storm blanket is gone, unzipped and put away. My sleeping bag has been unfastened down to my waist—thanks, Uncle Z. But wearing my outdoor parka and best hat and gloves, I'm still roasting. No sound of wind. The air smells crisp and clear. The storm's passed over completely. *Thank you, Saint Des!*

What time is it? How long have I slept? A long time, I reckon, and deeply. I feel very refreshed. The 'Vi's rocking to and fro, but it's not the wind, now. We're moving again.

I prop myself up on my elbow, wince as my chest twinges, then look around. The storm lights are still on, glowing at the bottom of the walls, and I can see Frankie and Myrrh, lying beside an empty bowl near the door, sleeping off a meal, no doubt fed them by Uncle Z to pre-empt them snacking on me. An indignant wriggle in response to my movement tells me that Gold is now curled up further down my sleeping bag, sleeping it off too. My lip quirks. I guess he left all his chicks to sleep together! He treats me like a man, now, more or less, but I guess in some ways I'll always be a chick, to him.

I touch the door panel. Six AM. When did the eye go over? Must've been hours ago. I'm so sweaty I oughta wash, but how long's Uncle Z been driving? I'd better offer to take the wheel straightaway. I check the view of the living area on the screen, but Star lies quietly, only a couple of blankets still draped over her. It's so much warmer already. It's only comparative, still below freezing, but still. I peel my hat and gloves off. It feels like spring. Spring at Christmas!

I ease out of the sleeping bag, trying to leave Gold undisturbed, but she jumps up and runs madly around the bedroom, inspecting everything and waking Frankie and Myrrh. As soon as I've lowered myself carefully out of the berth, I lift all three down before they can tumble from the doorway.

Star's breathing deep and even—her little three-clawed hands look okay, no sign of frostbite. Even emaciated, her vastly larger body mass gives her a huge advantage.

The chicks beat me into the cab. I send a stern maternal snarl after them and mebbe or mebbe not because of that they don't nip Uncle Z—thankfully, since the headlights blaze across a mountain face on one side and disappear into a precipice on the other.

"Hey, Uncle Z. Want me to drive?"

"When you've had some breakfast, yeah. But we've got a new problem."

"We're running out of the tranqs?"

"I said *new*." He takes one hand off the wheel for a moment and taps the fuel gauge.

I glance at it—then bend too quick to take a closer look, hissing in pain as I stare at the red bar. "What? Why the heck is it so low?"

"Think about it."

I do. It don't take long. "Star! All that extra weight. And then the storm—trying to heat the whole 'Vi! Heck, we must've burned through a ton of the stuff."

"Yep."

The main heater may be separate from the little cab blower, but it draws fuel from the same tank. "Are we gonna have enough?"

Uncle Z takes his time before replying. "Hopefully."

"Meaning?"

"We've been making good time since we got moving again. Ground's frozen so hard."

Yeah, the storm will have done us a favor, there.

Coming down into the lowland we'd normally be wallowing through mud and constantly re-routing around wet ground, this time of year. Thanks to the storm we can go straight over anything but deep water until it thaws, and that will take a few days at least, even at this lower elevation.

Uncle Z goes on, "In a few hours, we'll be at the highway, but there's no rest area with fuel for about three hours. But there's a camp in the foothills before we get to the highway. We can stop there and ask if they'll sell us some."

"Uninvited?" I shift uneasily. Going to a hunter's camp uninvited is a real no-no, unless you're closest of close friends.

"It's Christmas week. All the menfolk will be there. We know that and they know we know that, sure as sure. So it's rude, but it ain't vendetta-rude, if you get my drift."

"I s'pose." I try to call to mind the camp he means, and my heart sinks. "Uh, Uncle Z?"

"Yeah?"

"Ain't that Jason Desmoines' camp? His lot don't seem to like us much, him least of all. Never say a word to us, just sneer and mutter behind our backs."

"Yep."

"And, uh...ain't it Jason Desmoines that...well, when I was about eight, at the Midsummer's Eve gathering?

You punched him, then the two of you rolled around on the ground whacking each other until Dad and his brother pulled you apart?"

Uncle Z sighs heavily. "You remember that, do you?"

"Sure. When your folks tell you your whole life fighting's bad, then you see that, it's memorable."

"Yeah, I guess it is."

"And you think he's gonna sell us fuel? Help us out of a fix?"

"Since I'm none too sure we can reach the gas station, I think we have no choice but to ask. I mean, *I'd* sell *him* fuel in this situation, filthy weasel though he is, be wrong not to—so we'll just have to hope, right?"

"I guess." I eye Uncle Z for a moment. "Uncle Z?"

"Yeah?"

"Why *did* you punch him? You never would explain it."

Uncle Z's brown skin darkens as he blushes. "I shouldn't've, really. But...he called your Dad a hypocrite, and I flipped."

"A hypocrite? Who would think Dad was a *hypocrite*?"

Uncle Z hesitates again.

"C'mon, Uncle Z. I'm all grown-up. Surely you can explain it now?"

"Well... Your Dad called Jason out for bringing

some women to the 'Vi-park, and that's why Jason called your Dad a...a stinking hypocrite."

I'm not getting it. "Women visit hunters at the 'Vi-park sometimes. It's not that uncommon. I know it ain't good if they ain't married, but why did Dad single Jason out?"

"It was the reason why they were there," says Uncle Z. He rubs his finger and thumb together and I think I understand, though it makes me feel so dirty I wish I didn't. Well, I insisted I was old enough...

"Like a bad magazine, but worse?"

"Exactly. Much worse."

"Right. But why did he call Dad—" I break off, a cold lump forming in my stomach. "Because of me?"

Uncle Z nods, frowning like he's wishing he'd told me nothing, after all.

"But that's not fair! It weren't Dad's fault about me! It was that woman!"

"And that's why I punched him. But I shouldn't't've. Because your dad never went around telling everyone just how he came to have a son, did he? As if. So how was Jason to know any better? I wouldn't have done it if I hadn't had a beer. Isaiah was madder at me for that than about Jason—you know we agreed never to drink."

I nod.

"Well, that were the only time I broke it, and I

wished I hadn't. I did try to apologize, the next day, though it near killed me to do it to a weasel like that—but Jason weren't having any of it. Hated me ever since. Hated us all."

I sigh. The fight finally makes sense. "I guess I hope we can make it to the gas station."

"Yeah. Grab a bite to eat, then take over. Never mind speed, the new goal is fuel efficiency, 'kay?"

"'Kay."

"And wake me when we're nearly at Jason's camp."

"You bet." I don't want to speak to that man. He always looks at me like he's planning to skin me. Now that I finally know why, I almost wish I didn't.

DARRYL

Dad mutters something under his breath I'm obviously not supposed to hear and peers at the sky. Pre-dawn light should be filling the air by now, but what little we can glimpse through the blizzard is black as pitch.

"The eye can't be far away, Dad." My breath's misting in front of me, even with the car heater on full. "We need to get her with the others."

"Yes, but if she hasn't left that calf yet, she's not going to. Not in time." Dad raises his ScreamerBand to his wrist and presses the talk button. "Harry, are you done in the barns?"

Harry's voice comes from our bands: "Yeah, I was about to head back to the house."

"Bring the tractor and calf trailer out to Long Pasture, quick as you can."

"Okay."

Dad leaves the engine running to keep the heater on and starts peering out into the blizzard. He takes the heat scanner from me, quartering the area. "We'll take her to the barn," he says. "We don't want that dead calf attracting scavengers to the rest of the herd the moment the storm's gone over."

"Visibility's so bad, Dad, and the scanner's barely any use. Should you really go out-vehicle?"

"What carni'saur do you think's going to be abroad hunting in this?" But he carries on going over the landscape with the scanner, over and over, until the tractor looms out of the darkness, headlights blazing through the horizontal snowfall.

"Line it up with that dead calf, Harry," says Dad.

Once Harry's got it in position, Dad leaps out and dashes to the trailer while I carry on scanning the darkness for any threat. Quickly retrieving the winch sling from the back of the trailer, Dad jumps down again and slips it over the calf's ankle, bending double against the wind. The mare runs closer, her nostrils flaring, staring at him, but she's a good tame one, and she decides to give him the benefit of the doubt. He's careful to tuck himself out of sight behind the trailer before operating the winch, though, so she won't associate him with the calf being drawn away from her.

As soon as it's up on the trailer he staggers back to the truck, opens the door and topples back inside. For a moment he sits, shuddering with cold, then he gives himself a shake and beats his gloved hands together.

"Yep, it's nippy." Starting the engine, he drives right alongside the tractor. "Okay, you jump in the tractor and head back with Harry, help him get her into the barn. Don't worry about unloading or unhitching or anything, though, just get her in and get yourselves to the house. I'll check the last pasture and be right behind you."

I'm not sure what I like least, leaving Dad out here alone or leaving Harry to deal with an anxious four-ton mother alone. Arguing will only take up more time, so I do another quick thermal check, then pass the scanner to Dad, leap out and fight my way to the tractor, gripping the steps and hauling myself painstakingly up to the high cab as the gale tries to snatch me away. Harry opens the door and grabs the scruff of my jacket, dragging me in.

"Shut the door quick," he yells over the wind. "It's freezing!"

I'm all too happy to do so. The tractor's no warmer than the truck, and I'm shaking violently even after such a brief exposure to the storm. And I thought it was bad in the farmyard, in the shelter of the buildings.

Even crawling through the snow, it's not that long before we're drawing up to an empty 'saur handling barn. I jump out again and dash to the door controls, keeping an eye on the mother edmo, but she stays by the trailer, sniffing her calf. With the wind knifing through my layers as though I'm wearing a single T-shirt, a barn door has never seemed to open so slowly.

As soon as it's wide enough, Harry drives straight in, and the edmo follows. I close the door behind her and hurry to the human-sized door, flicking the barn heater on and climbing quickly to the obsoDeck. "Don't worry about anything else now, Harry," I call. "Let's get to the house."

"Okay." No argument there!

Harry's parked alongside the obsoDeck, so he can climb straight out the cab's roof hatch and pull himself up onto the deck. You never go down into a confined space with an animal that size. Ever.

I put my arm around Harry as we run to the house, towing him along. I don't *really* think he'll blow away—he's quite a big eleven-year-old—but the storm's so bad. Worst I've ever experienced. He doesn't object, so it must be freaking him out too.

But soon we're inside and I'm turning up the heating and putting the kettle on. Harry brings our quilts down to the family room so we can "penguin" through the worst bit. The "devil's inhale," that's what they call it further north—obvious enough why.

The wind hammers the closed shutters. The temperature's still dropping. Can't be long, now. I press my talk button. "Dad? Where are you?"

"I'm heading back, Darryl. Everything else is fine out here. Get the kettle on; I'll be there in a few minutes."

"Done that already. Be careful."

It's not until he's actually stepping through the door, stamping the snow from his boots, that I relax.

We settle with hot chocolate and cookies, quilts wrapped around us, and wait for that sudden, eerie silence to descend. Mom and Dad always tried to make the storms fun when we were little and Dad's carried on the tradition. Usually this part of a storm is a little scary but sorta fun—a change from routine, unplanned family time—but right now it just feels like it's one more thing ruining our Christmas.

This won't do. The storm isn't going anywhere; I need to get in the mood and make the most of it. We'll huddle, drink chocolate, eat cookies, and read aloud. Prayers and Bible stories, probably. It's what the storms make one feel like.

"Hah, I can hear myself think again," says Harry, trying for bravado as the ghostly peace finally begins.

But he draws Lion's cage a little closer, tucking the quilt around it to keep the featherless critter warm.

"And we can read, now." I pick up my new book from the sofa, but Harry grabs his tough book.

"*These* are much more suitable for a storm."

"What, you think Saint Des didn't survive storms?" I tease.

"Well, sure, but…" Harry looks appealingly at Dad, but Dad shrugs. He doesn't mind which.

I relent, though. Harry's prayer book probably does contain more relevant stuff right now. "Oh, go on, read from yours. Let's find out how hunters cheer themselves up through this sort of thing."

"With thoughts on their own insignificance and the absolute futility of doing other than entrusting themselves to the hand of God," predicts Dad, with a knowing smile.

"That sounds a bit grim," says Harry.

"Oh, they're not wrong," murmurs Dad.

"Go on, give it a try," I say. "Or I'll read from mine…" I raise it threateningly.

Hastily, Harry opens a page at random as the house begins to creak around us and reads, "Safety catches on, let's pray…"

Dad snorts faintly. Yeah, I bet hunters don't really say that, the book publisher just thought it sounded cool. Never mind. Let's pray...

The devil is inhaling.

JOSHUA

Uncle Z's taken the wheel as we approach the Desmoines' camp and he pulls around when we reach the gate, so we stop side-on to it, not nose-on like we're assuming we'll be let in, which would be super-rude. He peers towards the buildings for a moment, then presses the ping button on the Intercar unit to let them know there's someone here.

"Hello?"

A woman's voice. Darn. What if Jason and the guys *aren't* there? Two days after Christmas? Surely they are. They've got a pack of kids between them, right? Actually...yeah, I can see what Uncle Z was looking at. The indistinct shapes of two HabVis, heavily blanketed by the storm fall. They're here, alright.

"Could I speak to Jason, please, ma'am? It's Zechariah Wilson."

"I'll get him."

I stare at the camp with its encircling fence, far more solid than a farm fence, built to keep out people as well as 'saurs. Dad and Uncle Z might've settled somewhere like this, if they'd found ladies to marry. If they hadn't spent years hiding from the social workers who wanted to hand me to some perfect city family to raise in choking artificial fenced safety. Thank God they never caught us. I'm too old for them to be so interested, now, though we're still careful.

Uncle Z could still settle down, I guess. He's only three years older than Dad and Dad was only eighteen when I came along. He might still find some nice lady. And though there ain't no rule against women hunting, most of them don't want to. They want a house and a fence—city fence, farm fence, camp fence, but a fence. I don't see why anyone wants to live inside a fence, myself—I'd rather live in the 'Vi. But a farm or a camp ain't so bad. Not like a city.

The buildings cluster several hundred feet inside that solid fence, some bigger and in better repair than others. I think Jason and his brother and a cousin all have their families here, and so do the men they employ. Impossible to see what the yard looks like, with the snow blanketing everything.

Uncle Z drums his fingers on the wheel as he waits, an unusual sign of nerves, glancing at the fuel gauge as though hoping it will show something different. We've not done badly, but whether we've got another three hours' left...

"Zechariah?" Jason sounds mad already—uh-oh. "What the short-circuiting fences are you and your crazy nephew doing outside my place? 'Xactly when did I give you the impression you were welcome here? Just 'xactly how thick are you?"

"I know we ain't welcome, but we were hoping you'd fancy fleecing us by selling us some fuel for a healthy Christmas profit."

Silence. "You must need it bad, to show up *here*! You ain't invited! How dare you!"

Uncle Z bites his lip. "Come on, Jason, it's Christmas, we knew darn well you'd be at home. If the HabVis weren't here, we'd have driven right on."

"You need fuel. You really, really need it. Admit it."

"Yeah, sure we need it." Uncle Z grimaces, but there's no hiding it. Why else would we be here? "It's an emergency. Satisfied?"

"Satisfied? You've made my Christmas. 'Cos I get to say this. *Piss off*."

"Jason—"

"I mean it. You ain't getting none here."

"How about some tranquilizers? Hunters are meant to stick together, right? Sell us both at a huge mark-up and you can make a fine profit out of doing the right thing."

"No profit's worth more than the satisfaction of picturing you two stuck waiting for Highway Patrol." Jason spits the words. "The high and mighty Wilsons, waiting for Highway Patrol! It's priceless."

"Jason—"

"You had my answer. Now git yourself and your brother's rabid cub away from my fence 'fore I come out there and blow a hole in your tire. Or you."

Uncle Z grits his teeth. "You get what you give out, Jason, and Saint Des is listening. Have yourself a Merry Christmas."

He starts the engine and pulls away along the gravel track. But we haven't gone far when he slams a fist into the center of the steering wheel. Several times. "Heck, that, that—" He bites his lip, hard, his face darkening, sweat popping out on his forehead as he chokes back what he wants to say, his eyes darting to St. Des there on the dashboard. Determined all Saint Des's demerits should go to Jason, not him, no doubt.

"Vengeance belongs to the Lord," he mutters, eventually.

I keep quiet. Jason sure is one nasty weasel.

Finally, when I think Uncle Z might've simmered down a bit, I say, "The gas station it is, then?"

"Yeah. Gas station. Start praying."

DARRYL

By late morning the eye is long gone and the rest of the storm is blowing over. Our quilts are back on our beds, and Harry's working at taming Lion again.

I try to read my book, but Dad's words keep

popping back into my head: Hunters comfort themselves with "thoughts of their own insignificance and the absolute futility of doing other than entrusting themselves to the hand of God." They comfort themselves with that? And it *works*? How?

Father Benedict always says we're utterly insignificant in the eyes of the world but eternally significant in the eyes of God, but that's not what's niggling at me.

Oh... I've been so grumpy all Christmas, inside, because things haven't been going according to our plan. Okay, according to *my* plan. If I'd been thinking like a hunter, maybe I wouldn't have let it get to me so much. Maybe I'd have just gone with it. Accepted it. Made the most of it. I mean, I've been trying, but...I guess my efforts have been lacking... How exactly, Lord?

The answer swims up from the depths of me like a fish rising from a dark pool: *Somewhere in my response to everything that's happened has been lodged the idea that things should be revolving around me.*

Really? I feel like the fish has just leapt out of the water and slapped me in the face with its tail. Surely I don't think that, like...like some spoiled city-person! I know things don't revolve around me, right? I don't control my life, not really. Who does? If ever I needed a reminder of that, the storm provided one. And my life revolves around other things than *me*—the farm, our herds, Dad, Harry…

But all my fretting and fuming over Christmas hasn't been about any of that. Only about *my* Christmas. I mean, it's not like Dad or Harry was getting upset and acting like their Christmas had been ruined. It *was* about me.

What did Father Ben say, a while back? *Never underestimate the self-centeredness of any human being, least of all yourself.* I guess I nodded and accepted them as wise words, but didn't think they applied to me.

But they do. Somewhere inside me, there's a much bigger thread of selfishness than I realized. Nasty, hot shame fills me. If I've had a bad Christmas—and I *haven't*, not really—I've only myself to blame. I could've trusted and accepted and enjoyed what *was* much more, but I was too busy thinking about what wasn't.

I guess next time I see Father Benedict I'll confess to being selfish—and I'll finally believe it. My heart lifts, though, because I can imagine the sort of thing he'll say. *This is great, Darryl. You can't pull up a weed until you know it's there…*

Dad puts aside his hand-pad and goes out into the hall, distracting me from my thoughts. I put my book down and follow him. Sure enough, he's slipping his coat on.

"Going to take a look at the calf?"

"Yep."

I put my coat on and go with him. No more moping about my "perfect" Christmas. God's allowed everything that's happened for a reason and I need to trust that, even if I never know why.

The mother is losing interest in the calf now. It's still not moving and its scent is fading. We can get her back with her other calves soon. Right now, she's easy enough to lure away with a few treats and shut safely into the second pen, allowing us to go down to the trailer. We scrape snow from the carcass, which hasn't frozen too rock-hard thanks to the barn heater. Bloody gashes are soon revealed.

"Yep, raptors." Dad places his hand beside one, estimating the size. "Utahraptors."

The biggest raptor species and the largest carni'saur that can easily fit under the outer fence. Allosaurs could, but they'd have to duck and few animals will voluntarily get that close to an electric wire once they know what it is. Nothing smaller than a Utahraptor could take down a calf this well-grown. A pack of very hungry Dakotaraptors, maybe, but not normally. "But why didn't they eat it?" muses Dad.

I brush more snow away from the calf's belly. "Look, they started to. The storm, Dad! I bet they sensed the storm coming and ran for shelter."

"You're right. Well, my girl, we'd better zero your

new rifle this afternoon. We need to go hunting."

I grin, though I feel a touch of resignation. Yeah, that perfect Christmas really isn't happening this year. But I was already eager to adjust the sights on my new gun, and now Dad will help me get it just right.

I'm filled with the normal mixture of excitement and nerves at the thought of raptor-hunting. Which looks to be on God's Christmas activity schedule even if it wasn't on mine. I guess the only reason I wouldn't get enthusiastic about it would be if I thought I knew better than Him, right?

Huh, never thought about it quite like that before…

Hmm. Utahraptors. I can get enthusiastic about those, right? I mean, seriously good claws for my necklace and no mistake. Dangerous critters, though. Size and brains. Good practice entrusting myself to God's hand, then. Usually they stay away from fenced stock. Maybe it's a new pack—or a new matriarch is in charge.

Either way, we need to have a little chat about territory.

JOSHUA

My heart leaps when I see the sign—"Rest Area, 5 miles." We're so close. I glance at the fuel gauge. We're not quite out, yet.

I press the button to speak to the bedroom. "Uncle Z, we're nearly there." We've still got the tranquilizer problem—although we've been supplementing the dose with regular injections of various kinds of sedatives, we're down to our very last dose of proper tranquilizer—so we don't wanna waste a second at the gas station waiting for Uncle Z to get his pants on. He can go pay while I fuel up.

Uncle Z appears in the cab so quick I suspect he actually slept in them for once, though I don't bother trying to get him to admit it. He glances at the fuel gauge as well and settles into the passenger seat, shifting a dozing chick to one side to make room for his feet. "Good driving, Josh. We're gonna make it, no problem."

My cheeks go hot with pleasure. With Jason's insults still ringing in my ears, and after the marsh fiasco, his praise is so welcome.

The Rest Area info sign is coming up. My eyes narrow. There's a temporary sign screwed over it. What does it say?

Aw, no, no, no, no...

CLOSED FOR REFURBISHMENT
DECEMBER 24-30

Uncle Z swears. I stare numbly at the sign as it

passes us, then at the road ahead.

"Closed?" I say at last. "First gas station in about four hours, from the north, and it's *closed?*"

Uncle Z's biting his lip to keep from swearing again.

"How far to the next one?" I ask him urgently.

Grimly, he taps at the dash console, checking ahead on the route. "Two hours," he says flatly.

Two hours. "We're not gonna make that."

"Well, we're gonna have to try."

"We can't make that!"

"Oh, let me drive. *No,* don't waste the fuel stopping, just swap with me."

A little hurt to be displaced after he just complimented me on my fuel economy, I let him take the wheel. It's an awkward swap, with Star's tail in the way, Gold scrabbling, trying to stay on my lap, and my ribs hurting, but we manage it with only a few swerves. Not like there's many cars on the road—there's no one in sight at all.

Uncle Z nurses us along for almost another whole hour, then the engine starts coughing. He switches to the tiny reserve tank and we go another twenty minutes, then the coughing starts again. A few minutes later we're rolling gently to a halt on the emergency lane.

This is supposedly a "monitored highway" but out here in the wild north of the state—we're back in

Exception, now—the camera gantries are each about a mile apart and there ain't one in sight. If we were a city-car, they would log our failure to pass the next camera, of course. Though, even then, whether they'd automatically send a patrol car to check why the car had disappeared—the way they would in less remote areas—is debatable. But a HabVi? They'll assume we simply drove away off-road.

Uncle Z puts the emergency flashing lights on to signal that we need help. "Someone might come by," he says, "and let us have a little fuel. Only forty minutes to the gas station; we don't need much. Let's get up to the turret. We can start monitoring for carni'saurs and if anyone passes they'll be able to see us waving at them."

"Should we, uh..." I ease my way up the ladder, "if we get a lock-on, should we call Highway Patrol?"

There's a long silence as Uncle Z follows me up into the turret. Practicality warring with pride. "I guess we'd better," he says at last. "If there's any hope we won't have to shoot this allo in the end."

I let out a quiet breath in relief. Much as I cringe at the thought of waiting for Highway Patrol to bring us fuel, just like some hapless city-folk, my pride ain't worth any remaining chance of saving Star. I mean, we don't have to tell anyone it happened, right? Though I guess Jason's gonna tell everyone it happened, whether it does or not, so it don't hardly matter, now.

There's no satellite in range at the moment, so Uncle Z takes north and I take south and we start checking out the landscape. This way, if someone comes along, we'll already know if it's safe to get out and transfer some fuel.

"Nothing out there but a herd of chilly-looking stegosaurs," I say after a while. "And they're about a mile away."

"Well, let's hope they stay a mile away, seeing that we can't exactly drive off if one takes a dislike to us."

Yeah, good point. Huge, spiky tails on those things. Being out of fuel really stinks.

"Nothing over here, either," says Uncle Z. "Just a fox, hunting rodents under the snow. Oh, wait a minute, there's a car coming."

A car! Maybe we won't need to call Highway Patrol out!

We start waving—more and more wildly as it shows no sign of slowing. And then it's driving past and disappearing down the road.

"Why didn't they—" I groan and drop back into my seat. "Scared, I guess. But we wouldn't make *them* get out!"

"Mean and cowardly, you mean," mutters Uncle Z. "They know we'd be the first to stop and help them. But do they stop for us? Pah." He goes back to monitoring the landscape, so I do the same.

Eventually, another car comes, from the south. We wave again, and Uncle Z tries to hail them on the Intercar—but they drive on past. Uncle Z thumps the console. As though wanting to cheer him up, it chimes cheerfully.

Satellite-lock!

Uncle Z dives for it and is putting the call through in seconds.

"Hello, this is Highway Patrol, what is your emergency?"

"We're out of fuel."

"What is your position?"

Uncle Z reels off the coordinates, his face dark with embarrassment. He feels like some shame-faced city-kid, I guess. So do I.

"How many people in your party; men, women, children?"

"Myself and my nephew. Uh, he's sixteen." Yeah, in city-eyes, I *am* a child. Maybe they'll help us sooner, 'cos of that.

"What type of vehicle?"

"Uh..." Uncle Z's face—impossibly—turns even darker. "Uh, ah, a...it's a...a HabVi."

"Did you say a Habitat Vehicle?"

"Yeah. Did you know the only gas station in almost five hundred miles is flaming well *closed?*"

"People are always advised to check for travel

updates before making a journey," says the man, sounding like a robot as the words roll off his tongue. But he sounds more human—and *very* city-ish—as he adds. "If you hunters choose to ignore such basic safety procedures, you will get into trouble."

"Y'need signal to keep checking for—" Uncle Z breaks off, clearly remembering that we could lose this one any moment. "Look, we just really need some fuel. It's very urgent. Can you help?"

"Well, we don't have many patrollers in that area at the best of times and we've the minimum on duty over the holiday week. It's going to be a while, especially since you're in no danger from raptors or anything like that. A Habitat Vehicle is way down the priority list."

"Look, I get that, and normally we'd be happy to wait however long, but things aren't as simple as they'd usually be. We have an al— uh, we have a very large carni'saur in our vehicle, and we're almost out of tranquilizers. If we don't get fuel very soon it's gonna get loose and eat us."

"Really? You're going to let it eat you, are you? I think you mean if it gets loose you're going to shoot it and have nothing to sell. That's really not our problem. You do not count as high risk, and we'll get to you when we can."

I grab the mic from Uncle Z. "Look, the allosaur is a

mother, and we've got her three chicks on board. We're just trying to keep the family together. All we need is one can of fuel! They can chuck it out and drive straight on—"

"Did you say an *allosaur*? Aren't they almost as big as a T. rex? You can't fit an allosaur in a Habitat Vehicle! And *chicks*? At this time of year? Look, you two, just wait your turn. And I suggest you try to sober up before the patrol car arrives—because I'm going to make sure you're both breathalyzed. Good day." There's a click as the call is disconnected.

I stare at Uncle Z in dismay. "Did I just make things worse?"

"Aw, they were never gonna come in time. Not once they knew we were hunters. If anything," he actually grins, "they might come quicker now, if they think they can get me for drink-driving and you for underage drinking. Won't they be disappointed, heh?"

We go back to watching the landscape. Two more cars pass, but they both pretend not to see us waving or hear what we're saying on the InterCar, keeping their eyes on the road ahead and accelerating as though they think they'll be eaten simply for pulling over.

Dang city-folk.

Dang city-folk in their little cars full of lovely fuel...

"We shoulda pulled to a halt across the roadway," I

mutter. "Then they'd have to stop!"

Uncle Z snorts bleakly.

Through the open hatch, I see Star's leg twitch. Not for the first time, but that was a bigger movement. She's getting less and less thoroughly tranqued by the hour. I tap Uncle Z's shoulder and point down to her. He grimaces.

"Okay, cover me while I give her some more sedative," says Uncle Z softly. "The last dose of proper tranqs might just get us from here to the zoo, if we put our foot down real hard, but no longer. So we can't give it to her until we're actually ready to move. So from now on, we tip-toe around, we speak very very soft and only when necessary, and we try to avoid food smells— no cooking. No treading on her tail to get into the cab— I know that's hard for you with a sore chest, but try. And above all, we don't move an inch around this vehicle without our rifles—and our earpieces. Okay?"

I nod. We'll try to remove all stimulus for her to wake up, just keep her lying there, all calm and sleepy and content. She's so hungry, though, it ain't gonna work long and the sedatives don't actually put her under...

I rest my forehead in my hands for a moment, helplessness gnawing at me.

Dad, help us? Pray for us, please?

Slinging my rifle over my shoulder, I follow Uncle Z below.

DARRYL

I carry the target back to where Dad and Harry are waiting and hold it up. "I'd say we're done."

Dad takes it from me and admires the little cluster of holes in the center. "Perfect. You happy to go after those rogue raptors tonight?"

I refuse to hesitate. So what if this is turning into one heck of a Christmas week: rescuing Father Ben, staying up all Christmas night, the storm? So what if what I really want is to crash out for a bit? It's not about me, and God's got this.

"'We'd better had." The raptors barely got to eat any of that calf. So there's a real danger they'll come back for another. Or the same one. If we put it back where they expect to find it we can simply lie in wait. I glance at Harry. "You game?"

"Yeah, I want some Utahraptor claws! They're, like, nine inches long!"

"Only if you take down a large female," says Dad. "Okay, let's load the hunting truck and sort out our ammo. Then we can chill until chores."

Chilling, chores, and a raptor hunt. Just a normal Christmas day on a farm, right?

JOSHUA

We wave to a couple more passing cars and watch the landscape, but little changes. No one stops. No sign of Highway Patrol. Is this really gonna end with Star dead? So much for her being Saint Des's Christmas gift. Guess we got that wrong. At least we can get the chicks to the zoo. Assuming we don't mis-time it when it comes to shooting Star, and get ourselves eaten. Impossible to put her out of the vehicle now. Even the last "proper" dose of tranquilizers we're saving is smaller than is safe for actually unchaining and handling her.

Come on, Saint Des, Dad, God. Help?

With a peep of exertion, Gold belly-flops into the turret, then stands up, shaking her downy feathers into place, looking pleased with herself. She's been trying to get up the ladder for over an hour, since it became clear I wasn't coming down any time soon, but Uncle Z didn't want me to bring her and her little teeth up here, though she hasn't bitten him recently. "You finally made it, huh," I murmur, very softly, following it up with a congratulatory chirrup.

She springs straight into my lap and curls up. With the heater out of action, it's not that hot down there, though the occasional ray of sun is warming the turret a little. Frankie and Myrrh are still wearing their hat-coats. They ought to all be alright, really, with their feathers, even Gold, after all the food they've had in the last few days, but Gold's clearly getting used to her comforts. I stroke her gently and she arches her neck, positively enjoying the sensation by now and making happy sounds.

Uncle Z glances around, raises an eyebrow and snorts—also very softly. Then turns his attention back to the road. "If someone don't come in the next half hour," he says quietly, "We'd better shoot the allo. Then we can haul her out and leave her here."

"We could give her the last dose," I say. "Buy us some more time."

Uncle Z turns to me. "Josh. There's no point burning fuel carting two and a half tons of allo along with us when we darn well know we'll never be able to get her there alive."

"But we could get more drugs, mebbe. When we got further south."

"You can't just walk into a city vet and buy those drugs, Josh, y'know that. You have to be registered with the supplier."

"But—"

"It's getting too dangerous, Josh. We tried, okay? But it's you or the allo, now, and that ain't a difficult decision for me."

I say nothing. We did try. But we've almost failed.

I carry on stroking Gold as the minutes tick by, my

eyes roaming over the grassland, searching, searching. It's so *frustrating*. We tried so *hard*. But there ain't any more we can do.

Saint Des, this really is up to you, now. You and the Almighty.

"*If you take our breath, we return to earth, and our plans this day come to nothing,*" I murmur.

Uncle Z shoots me another look over his shoulder. "I am sorry, Josh." He checks the time. "Look, that's half an hour. I'll go take care of it, okay?"

Not okay, but what else can we do? He's the boss, anyway. "I'll take over monitoring your sector as well," I mutter.

"Good man." Uncle Z settles his rifle over his shoulder and swings onto the turret ladder as I turn my eyes north, taking stock of the land, the possible cover, the danger points...

"Hey, there's a vehicle coming!" I speak a little too loud in my excitement.

Uncle Z steps back up to join me, and we watch the speck approaching. It's a black van, we see as it comes closer. And as it comes closer still, we can make out the white dorsal stripe running from the middle of the hood, along the roof, and presumably down to the rear bumper.

"Huh, an SOS van," says Uncle Z. "Is he a Pharisee or a Samaritan, I wonder?"

I've a vague idea what he means, from the Bible stories Dad used to read with me. I start to wave long before the driver's close enough to see me. This is Star's last chance.

Eventually Uncle Z starts waving too. The vehicle loses speed as it approaches. That's a first. I glimpse a face darker than Uncle Z's peering out. It's going slow...but the vehicle passes us. My heart plummets—until it pulls neatly onto the emergency lane and reverses to stop just ahead of us. Someone who actually knows the safe parking order on an emergency lane, for a wonder—largest vehicle at the back.

Our Intercar crackles, then a friendly voice speaks.

"You guys okay? Can I help?"

DARRYL

I didn't chill much, when it came to it, because I realized it's the Feast of the Holy Family today. We have our family traditions for all the meals in the Christmas Octave, and this is one of my favorites. I'm not letting raptors or the storm spoil this one, too—not unless the Lord has something else planned, anyway!

Roast beef—from our own herd—and roast potatoes—peeled by Harry—are in the oven. Harry's stirring the gravy, looking grumpy 'cos he was hoping to slip away until it's time to eat. Dad's gone to drive the fence early, so we can head straight out to hunt after what'll have to be a rather early meal.

In wild areas raptors hunt by day as often as by night—but they usually wait for darkness to creep close to human habitations, if they've any experience of people at all. We need to be waiting for them.

The hunting truck's ready. We just need to tow the calf back to the pasture, then get in position nearby. With night scopes, we could probably take out most of the pack before they realized what was happening, but we don't plan to slaughter them all. We'll just take out two or three, depending on whether we all hit one, then switch the high powered lights on full. And the horn. And the ultrasonic repellers on the inner fence. Scare the heck out of them. Once the survivors have run under the outer fence, we'll switch on the repellers there, too. Leave them on a day or two, to make the lesson stick.

We'll have to switch them off again, after that. They play havoc with all the wildlife if you run them continually—and they start to wind up the mares. Some people reckon raptors can simply get used to them if they're always on, as well.

I take stock of the meal preparations. I'm not into fancy cooking, usually, though I often go to more effort than Dad. I've done carrots and peas. I remember Mom used to do so many types of veggies and stuff for meals like this, but there's a limit to how many things I can juggle. The batter is mixed ready, so I can pour it into the little dishes heating in the oven as soon as Dad gets back, to make the yorkie puddings.

We may have missed our Saint Stephen's Day meal, but we're not going to miss our British feast tonight—Lord willing!

JOSHUA

"I can offer food, water, absolution...?" continues the voice, cheerily.

Uncle Z already has the Intercar mic to his lips. "We just need fuel. If you could let us have some of that... We can pay."

"Fuel? Sure." The—presumably—priest sounds deeply relieved. "That's an easy one. I wasn't looking forward to trying to fix something you guys already couldn't fix with all the tools you've no doubt got in there, that's for certain."

"Yeah, we're just out of fuel," says Uncle Z. "You don't need to get out. We've got a siphon pump; I can take care of it."

"Sure. I'm getting a little low, but there's enough to get us both to the next gas station. The last one was closed, can you believe?"

"Yeah, we noticed that," says Uncle Z grimly.

"Thought you might've. Well, I'll push the button to unlock the fuel cap and you can take what you need."

His eyes glinting with hope, Uncle Z gives me a big thumbs-up that I return and swings onto the ladder, tip-toeing down it. I quickly check all around the surrounding area again while Uncle Z fishes out the fuel siphon from a locker with painstaking care, trying not to make a sound.

No sign of danger. Not out *there*.

"All clear, Uncle Z." I speak softly—he'll hear it through his earpiece.

"Good." He could most easily exit through the cab doors without letting the chicks out, but he'd have to climb over Star's tail again. Access is simpler to the side door, so he simply closes it behind him double-quick and walks over to the van.

"Thanks a heap for stopping. You won't believe how many people just drove straight on by— Hang on, do I know you? Uh...Father...Ben, was it? We met at that breach down in Rado state, about, uh—" For some reason he glances up at me in the turret. "—about seventeen years ago, right?"

"Well, I never. What was the name? Zachariah?"

"Zechariah, but yeah."

"Well, you're a long way from home."

"Nah, we relocated to Exception not long after that. Isaiah always hoped we'd run into you some time."

I can just glimpse the priest's face at the van's driver's window as he peers back at the 'Vi. "Is that Isaiah up there?"

Uncle Z's silent for a beat before answering. "No. No, that's my nephew. Isaiah's boy, Joshua."

"Oh, he looks real like him from here."

"Yeah, and" — I just catch Uncle Z's next words, soft and mysterious — "I reckon you know exactly how he came into the world, though you can't ever admit it to anyone."

The priest continues as though Uncle Z hadn't spoken, "And, uh, your brother?" The priest's voice is tense, now, like he's sensing what's coming.

Uncle Z shakes his head.

"Ah, darn. I'm sorry to hear that. I liked him. What happened?"

I try not to listen as Uncle Z tells it in a couple of sentences, focusing instead on giving the landscape another going over. I don't wanna be sad right now, when suddenly we have hope again.

"I really would love to catch up," says Uncle Z, soon enough, "but we've got a real large carni'saur in there and we're running real low on tranquilizers, so we're almost as short on time as we are on fuel."

"Sure, I understand. Grab some and get moving."

Uncle Z goes to the van's open port and feeds one end of the siphon into the tank. He puts the other end into our own tank and starts the pump. "Josh, come down to the cab and tell me when we've got enough. We don't wanna take too much and strand Father Ben instead. But we're gonna lose a chick if I keep coming in and out."

"Okay." I give the landscape one more going over. Nothing. I can safely go below for a few minutes. Well—if "below" currently counts as "safe." Arranging my rifle very carefully over my shoulder so it won't chink against the rim of the hatch, and tucking Gold inside my coat to save her from falling down the hole as soon as I'm gone—she stretches sleepily and settles again—I lower myself stealthily down the ladder, looking over my shoulder at Star the whole time.

Her head moves slightly as I reach the bottom. One massive eyelid slides back, exposing a huge, amber eye. I stand motionless, trying not to breathe. Heck, she's too awake. Please God she's feeling too dopey to pay attention or do anything. Soon as we've got the fuel on board, we can tranq her properly again. Or as properly as can be achieved with too small a dose. But anything will be better than this.

"Josh? Are you coming?" Uncle Z's voice in my ear again. I carry on standing still.

Star's eyelid slides shut again. Her foreclaw twitches slightly. Her breathing slows a little. Dozing? I tip-toe to the cab doorway and stare at the mass of tail filling the gap. I cannot touch her tail... Not right now. Forcing myself to ignore my chest, I grab whatever I can on each side of the door jam and swing monkey-style onto the driver's seat. *Ow-ow-ow-ouch.* But no tail-contact.

Uncle Z's peering up at the cab. I point towards Star and make an "eye-open" gesture, grimacing. Uncle Z's face tenses in concern, but he jerks his head to the fuel gauge, motioning me to hurry. In the very latest HabVis, absolutely everything can be controlled from any console, but in a slightly older vehicle like this the engine systems are still separate. It doesn't usually matter.

I let the gauge come up a bit more, then give Uncle Z a "kill" gesture. He removes the siphon and closes the ports, speaking to the priest. "I think both vehicles have enough, now, but we'd better drive to the gas station together, to be sure. We owe you some fuel, anyway."

"Ah, don't worry about that," says the priest. "Christmas gift. But I'm all for driving together. I wouldn't want to be stranded twice in one week. Be a shame to let raptors rip my van to bits again after a very kind community further south just put it back together for me. You've them to thank for the fact that I'm driving along here today, you know."

"Then I hope Saint Des blesses them for it," says Uncle Z.

Yeah. Maybe he'll even use *us* to do *them* a good turn, someday. He does that kinda thing.

"Your van sure does look like it took a beating recently," adds Uncle Z. "Wish we could stop to hear about it, but our carni'saur is waking up, big time."

"Let's get going, then."

Uncle Z opens the side-door again and slips in. Frankie tries to dart past him, but he lunges and grabs him, prodding the door close button with his elbow. The door closes safely, but Frankie screeches and struggles. Uncle Z releases him hastily, but from where I kneel on the driver's seat, I see Star's huge eyelid snap up. Oh boy, she heard Frankie...

Her jaws open wide—the muzzle snapping and twanging off across the room—and she bellows her maternal wrath, the sound rebounding off the metal walls like hammer-strokes on the ears. Then, with a *snap-crack-twang* of breaking metal, she raises her head half a foot—Uncle Z was right about these chains being too weak. Her tail flexes, sending Myrrh tumbling across the cab floor.

I start to scramble across to the passenger seats, meaning to lift Myrrh up onto them, out the way—but Star's tail rises, lashing viciously in the confined space, smacking against the raptor-proof windows—and knocking me down into the gap I'm trying to cross.

Squeezed between Star's tail and the seat, I attempt

to extract myself but only end up sliding down as her tail flexes, ending up underneath it. The weight settles across my thighs, crushing me to the ground. Only the force of life-long training stops me yelling out in pain like a juicy piece of prey.

"Quick, Uncle Z, tranq her!" I whisper instead.

"I'm working on it!"

But it's gonna be dangerous for him to tranq her, without cover. I grab hold of a seat strut and pull, wriggling, struggling to get free, but she's too heavy.

Uncle Z must hear me panting. "What's going on in there; you okay?"

"She's got me pinned, but I'm not in danger, just tranq her quick!"

"Gimme a moment, I'm gonna have to use the dart gun."

Yeah, who wants to get close enough to put an injection in her gum, now she's this wide awake?

Star roars again, struggling against the straps in earnest, rocking the entire vehicle. I try even harder to get free but it's no use.

I almost jump out of my skin when a face appears at the passenger window, peering in, eyes widening at the sight of the huge tail. It's the priest, Father Ben. He got out of his vehicle? Gutsy guy.

He points at the door lock. Right...

Stretching, I just manage to reach the button. He

opens it and climbs in—"Careful, don't let her pin you, too..."—but he's scrambled straight up onto the passenger seats. He slams the door and presses back against it, shielding his face with his arms as Star's tail lashes around again. I make another attempt to get out of the gap between the seats, but the base of the tail simply ain't moving as much and keeps me pinned. *Argh!*

"Short-circuiting power lines! Large carni'saur? That's a— That's—" As Father Ben shakes off his astonishment and leans down to grab my wrists, a whiff of incense tickles my nose—making a nice change from angry allo scent. "Here, let me see if I can—" He braces a foot against the dashboard and pulls.

He's big and strong, and slowly I slide free, grabbing my rifle even as I leap up onto the seat. "Thanks! I've gotta help Uncle Z." I scoop Myrrh from the floor—where he cowers from the lashing tail, looking dazed—and shove him at the priest. "Here, try and stop him getting squashed! Grab the other one if you can. They don't bite—much," I add over my shoulder, as the startled priest holds the squirming chick out at arm's length.

I leap over Star's tail, through into the living area, no worry about touching it now, just getting over it before it can move again and squish me against the wall. I'm dimly aware of the priest following me, still clutching Myrrh, but I'm too busy looking around. Uncle Z crouches in the corner, a syringe in one hand, just putting aside the empty tranquilizer bottle and picking up a dart ready to fill it.

Star's head is still mostly fastened down—I spoke ill of the chains too soon. Most are still holding—just. But her body is twisting and thrashing as she tries to break free. I can see straps fraying, chain links twisting, stretching, about to part...

I glance at Uncle Z again. By the time he's filled the dart and got it into the gun—Star's gonna be loose. We have about fifteen seconds left to do it the old way or we'll just have to shoot her.

I don't give Uncle Z a chance to argue. I drop my rifle, snatch the syringe from his hand, dart forward and leap.

"No, Josh!"

Too late. I've landed on the back of her neck, her crest feathers brushing my nose, my arm outstretched, the needle plunging straight into her gum. I'm pressing the plunger. *Going in, going in, going in—* Her neck jerks viciously against the chains...

Snap! The links part and her head whips through the air, throwing me off. I slam against the wall, back first, hard enough to bruise a few more ribs. Sliding down, I land in the gap between her neck and the wall, smothering gasps of pain and fighting to stay still.

Star's head is feet away, though facing away from me, thank God. Still raised, but it sways. Her eyes blink slowly. She's still real groggy. She could just turn her head and grab me, but mebbe she won't notice me... My heart hammers in my chest, painful-hard.

Uncle Z's raising his rifle purposefully, about to shoot. Mebbe he doesn't realize I got it in—most of it. We've just gotta wait... I raise my hand, just a tiny bit, palm flat. *Don't.*

His jaw tightens, and he don't lower the gun, but he don't shoot, either, just holds his aim, providing cover. The priest stands, eyes wide with horror, Myrrh still under one arm, but he now has Frankie tucked under his other arm, for a wonder. Guess he actually took in what I said.

Inside my jacket, Gold shifts restlessly. I managed not to squash her too hard against Star's neck, but hitting the wall must've woke her. If she makes a sound... *Quiet, Gold, quiet! Don't get me or your mom killed, please!* But I'm still, now. Mebbe she'll just go back to sleep...

I keep breathing very slow and shallow. It's easy to ignore the pain, with this much adrenaline flooding me...

Star's nostrils twitch. How long before this starving allo realizes there's a hunk of warm meat lying just behind her? Her head turns from side-to-side slightly, her eyes blinking. Groggy and confused. Looking for her chicks? It's all so unfamiliar in here; she probably can't make sense of anything in her current state.

How long until the drug works?

Come on, Star. You've still got a ton of that other stuff in you. You must feel super-relaxed...

If singing a lullaby would help, I'd do it, but all I can do is stay still—and pray. *C'mon, Saint Des, make the drugs work! Get her to sleep before she eats me or Uncle Z shoots her.*

Each moment ticks slowly by in a silence broken only by Star's heavy breathing and the odd grumpy peep from Frankie and Myrrh. Star's still peering that way, but her head's swaying more. She's stopped struggling against the straps that hold her body down. Her eyelids droop.

That's right... Sleep, girl...

Finally, her head drops to the ground. She blinks a few more times, then her breathing slows and deepens. Eventually, I dare to ease stiffly to my feet. I have to go right around her head to get out from behind her—that or climb over her, but the last thing I want is to wake her up again. My foot nudges the fallen syringe so I pick it up and take it with me to Uncle Z. The needle's snapped off, but it's almost empty.

"See, Uncle Z. She had almost all of it. We can give her the rest later."

He just grabs me and shakes me hard. He stops when I gasp in pain, but ooh, he's mad! *"Not cool, Joshua! You should've let me handle it!"*

I shrug guiltily. "Yeah, but...Star would be dead..."

"I'd rather Star was dead fifty times than you were nearly dead once," he snaps. "And that"—he jabs a finger in my chest—"was you nearly dead! Don't you dare do anything like that again! Don't you like being alive?"

"Yeah, I do! I was safe enough. If she'd seen me, you'd've shot her."

"Safe? Oh, come on, Josh, you know how fast a critter like that can move!"

"Sure, one that hasn't spent the last few days being pumped full of every tranquilizer and sedative in the 'Vi..."

"Ah, heck, you survived, she's flat-out; why are we wasting time? Let's get her to the dang zoo!"

"I'll say!" More tetchy noises from the male chicks, and I turn hastily to the priest. "Oh, put them down, quick. They sound fed up, and they don't know you." He deposits them on the ground one by one, still looking a bit stunned. "Thanks for looking after them," I add.

"Uh, glad I could help." The priest runs a hand over his tight, curly hair, eyeing Star's bulk. "I didn't even know you could fit one of those in a vehicle."

"It sure ain't the norm," says Uncle Z. "And I can't say I'd recommend it, after this. Look, we need to put our foot down. There was barely enough in that syringe to keep her under until we reach the zoo."

"Well, that's not good. Let's move, then."

Uncle Z hurries up the turret to check the coast is clear for the priest to return to his van—two could do it quicker but he eyes me and tells me to stay below, which I'm glad of since my ribs at the back now feel about the same as my ribs at the front and both together don't feel very good at all. But no question of pain pills. Not the time to be woozy.

I give Father Ben a quick version of the Allosaur Zoo Express saga while we wait.

"You were out in the storm?" He shakes his head. "Rather you than me. It was a bad one."

I shrug. "They're no fun, but you can't come north without running into them, now and then."

I'm still eyeing the priest with a mixture of curiosity and wariness. When I was little, if any city-person came to the 'Vi-park unexpectedly—priest, city official, cop, whatever—Dad and Uncle Z would leave if they could or hide me in a cupboard if leaving didn't seem prudent. If someone was expected, we simply wouldn't be there, period. I only saw priests properly twice a year when we went to church at Christmas and Easter.

But Dad finally admitted to Uncle Z that he'd done

a DIY baptism on me when I was a baby but he was worried sick in case he'd not got it right. So they took me to that Father Morris when I was five, to arrange a proper one. They thought I was old enough he'd be okay about me living in the 'Vi. Didn't end well. They had a physical tug-of-war over me in the church car park, the priest yelling that the 'Vi wasn't safe and I had to stay in-city. Dad and Uncle Z won and we fled into Yoming and didn't return to Exception until it was clear the authorities weren't actively looking for me. But we never dared set foot in a church again, in case someone reacted the same way.

Though I'm sure they used to assume I'm just out on some temporary little hunting trip, the priests I've seen around the 'Vi-park since I got a bit older have mostly seemed okay. And this guy knew Dad...

In fact, his eyes have just fixed on our photo frame and he's taken a step towards it.

"Ah, there's Isaiah." His finger hovers over the screen. "And that's you? You were a cute baby."

I roll my eyes. Why do people always say stuff like that?

"I recognize that 'Vi, too," Father Ben says, as the picture changes.

"Yeah, it's our old one."

He turns to me again. "I liked your dad. We had quite an adventure together, though I dare say it was all in a day's work for him. I'm really sorry for your loss."

I shrug and look away, my chest tight and hurting. "He didn't do anything stupid. Guess it was just his time."

The priest smiles sadly. "You must miss him."

"Loads. But I've got Uncle Z. We're okay."

"Yeah. That's good."

Gold begins to wriggle, so I unzip my jacket to let her put her head out, making the priest's eyes widen. "Another chick! Doesn't it bite you?"

"Nah. Not anymore." I stroke Gold under the chin and croon softly to keep her calm. She smells of warm chick and eager energy, but there's no point letting her out when Father Ben will be opening that door in a moment. "Want to feed her? Then she might let you pet her. You've got the right vibe."

"Hmm." He eyes Gold. "Far bigger teeth than a piranha'saur, there." But he holds out his hand and lets me drop a little training treat onto it, then offers it to Gold, keeping his palm good and flat without needing to be told, so that the food stands out clearly.

Gold stares at his hand for a moment, nostrils flaring at his strange scent, but finally darts her head out and takes the tidbit. "There, see," I tell her. "He's a nice human." I re-enforce the message with some approving allo-noises and glance at the priest. "You can try and pet her now. I think she'll let you."

"You don't *have* to, Father." Uncle Z's dry voice floats down from the turret, though I bet his eyes don't stop inspecting the landscape. "Josh sometimes struggles to understand that not everyone's idea of fun is getting cozy with something that would like to eat him."

"Gold don't want to eat us," I object. "Not unless we run out of food."

Uncle Z snorts.

I shoot an uncertain look at Father Ben. "I weren't making you feel like you have to, was I? She might nip you—it is true. But I thought you knew that."

Father Ben grins. "I do know that. And despite whatever reservations I expressed about her teeth, it'd be something to have petted an allo, even a little one. Can I?"

"Sure!" I carry on crooning and stroking Gold gently under the chin as Father Ben reaches out to her. "Let her smell you first..."

Gold sniffs his hand with interest. Her teeth part slightly, but I give her a firm "no" and a disapproving rumble, so she sits there looking innocent as he runs a hand down the back of her neck.

"She's soft."

"Yep."

"Okay, sorry to break up the petting zoo," Uncle Z's voice interrupts us. "Check's complete—it's safe out there. Let's move."

"Oh, you'd better go."

"Yeah," says Father Ben. "Well, thanks."

"Huh? Thank *you*." If he hadn't come to help I'd probably have been stuck under Star's tail while she and Uncle Z killed each other. To say nothing of the fuel.

He traces a quick blessing over me and Gold, then another up towards the turret.

"Clock's ticking," calls Uncle Z, oblivious.

I get hold of Frankie and Myrrh, and off Father Ben goes out the side door. "Thanks!" I call again, as it slides shut behind him.

We cruise to the gas station in convoy—at best fuel-efficiency speed since another halt to transfer fuel in either direction will delay us far more—and fill up at adjacent pumps, but there's no time to waste on more chit-chat. Uncle Z and I leap back into the 'Vi the moment we're done, leaving Father Ben still waiting in line to pay.

Uncle Z chuckles as we pull away.

"He gonna find it's paid for, ain't he?" I say.

"Sure is. Least we can do."

"I'll say."

"Okay, can you take the wheel for a bit? How bad are you hurt? Don't tell me you ain't; I saw how hard you hit that wall and the way you're standing since."

"It's just bruises. Nothing cracked this time. I can drive for a few hours." We both know Uncle Z needs to take the wheel full-time once we get further south. Busier highways, more chance of getting pulled over. City-folk have this thing about driver's licenses and they give them out according to age rather than ability.

"Okay. I'll put my head down for a couple of hours. Wake me if you get tired or you need to stop."

"Sure. Oh, can you feed the chicks first? They look hungry."

Soon I'm driving along the highway in the mid-afternoon light at a ridiculously un-fuel-efficient-and-not-entirely-legal speed while the chicks squabble over a bowl of meat. I know when they've finished eating because Gold hops back up onto my lap.

I stroke her feathers now and then as I drive, talking to her in allo and in human speak. "I'm gonna miss you, little golden girl. Will you miss me too?" She raises her head, checking my fingers for treats. Finding nothing, she settles down again. "I guess not. You'll have all the food you need and a nice warm mom to cuddle up to, and probably heat lamps, too. Ah well, let's get you there, quick as we can."

I keep driving, on and on, as the sun begins to drop in the sky. We're still in a race against time.

DARRYL

The British pudding is my favorite part of the Holy Family supper. Everyone's, I think. And because we didn't have our rum bomb, we're going to enjoy it twice as much this year. So I guess all that feeling like we were missing out and feeling sorry for myself really was stupid.

I carry the pudding carefully from the kitchen on a plate held with oven mitts, steaming hot, and Dad pours brandy over the top while Harry rushes to get the lights.

Whump! Dad strikes a match and the brandy ignites, pretty blue flames licking up around the dense, spherical pudding as I give an involuntary "ooh" and Harry keeps up an excited commentary.

"Father Ben says it's what gave Mrs. Grierson part of the idea for the rum bombs," Dad tells us, the way he always does, as the flames die down and Harry turns the light on again, the aroma of caramelized fruit heavy in the air. "Brits do this on Christmas Day, you know."

"It's awesome!" says Harry. "Why don't we?"

Dad shrugs. "Well, some people do, nowadays, don't they? But we've got plenty of Christmas Day traditions of our own. How many desserts can even you eat in one day?"

"I guess."

We devour large bowlfuls of the super-sweet fruity

pudding with gobs of rum butter, brandy butter, and cream. Yum!

Then it's time for my second-favorite British import—Christmas crackers. I offer my decorated cardboard cylinder to Dad and he takes the other end while offering his to Harry. Once I've grabbed the free end of Harry's cracker, the circle—well, triangle—goes all the way around. Then, we pull! They split with sharp cracks of exploding gunpowder, spilling paper hats, gifts, and slips of paper with silly jokes onto the table.

"What do you call a one-eyed dinosaur?" reads Harry, clutching his joke slip in one hand while cramming his paper hat on with the other.

"Do-you-think-he-saurus," Dad and I chorus.

"Oh, come on," says Dad, "They've got to do better than that!"

But all too soon, Dad's shooting a look out the window at the darkening sky. Our Christmas fun needs to give way to duty. We've a herd to protect.

We replace our paper hats with woolly ones—and coats and mittens, since we could be out all night, for all we know—and pick up our rifles.

The Utahraptors don't care that it's the Feast of the Holy Family. But maybe the Holy Family will smile on us tonight.

And as far as Christmas fun goes, there's still quite a few days of the Christmas Octave left, right? And

even longer until twelfth night. Plenty of time to relax—
or to enjoy whatever the Lord has planned.

Christmas isn't over yet!

JOSHUA

I sleep for quite a few hours after Uncle Z takes over,
but I'm awake and back in the cab as we drive through
the goods entrance of Yoming Central Zoo at about ten
minutes to midnight. There's a sense of unreality to this
arrival, like a small miracle!

I glance at our little Saint Des statue on the
dashboard, which survived the ravages of Star's
thrashing tail untouched, no surprise. *Thank you, Saint
Des!*

Star grunts and shifts in her sleep as we maneuver
through the zoo—if it still counts as sleep. She's been
getting less and less deeply unconscious for the last
hour. We've given her another big dose of sedatives, but
we're staying quiet as mice in the cab. Every time a
chick wakes up I toss it some more food to settle it off
again, double-quick. They've got plenty of weight to
make up, so it won't hurt them.

We've had a smooth run since parting from Father
Ben, except just once about four hours ago when a cop
car pulled Uncle Z over for speeding. Uncle Z made
them park behind us and opened our back door to show

them Star, still lying there half-unchained with her broken muzzle beside her, and they didn't even write him a ticket. I dunno if they put out word to leave us alone, but we ain't been stopped again though we didn't slow down any.

As we draw to a halt in what looks like the carni'saur handling pen complex, four people come out of a nearby cabin, so we're in the right place. A couple of keepers, a vet, and the inevitable eager young intern, by the look of it. We sent them our ETA earlier when we got another signal-lock—we updated Highway Patrol, too. Didn't sound like anyone was even on route to us yet. Thank God for Father Ben.

The allo welcome party crowd around, but Uncle Z puts a finger to his lips, waving them into silence before opening his window and handing the nearest guy a tranquilizer dart.

"Quiet!" He speaks under his breath. "Load this up right away. The allosaur is barely asleep back there; we ran out of drugs. We need to tranq her properly before we do a thing with her."

The zoo staff recoil from the vehicle, staring as though wondering if it will contain a wide-awake allosaur. But a few quick—and quiet—words from the lady keeper and the intern gallops off clutching the dart.

"Barely asleep?" murmurs the male keeper. "Heck."

"Shhhh," says the woman, more sensibly.

Silence falls until the intern returns. Everything goes smoothly after that, for a wonder. We dart Star, wait fifteen minutes, then run a cable through the ring on the wall of their chosen handling pen and haul her out. I fetch Frankie and Myrrh—now hiding in the cab from all the strangers—and hand them over, still in their little coats.

"Oh, d'you want your hats back, Uncle Z?"

"Never mind," says Uncle Z, then turns to the keepers, "you'd better keep the allo tranqued for a while and the chicks close by her so they have a chance to smell right again. We came through a storm and had to keep them warm any way we could. They must stink of human, by now. Or better still," he adds, since the vet is frowning in concern, "since she's been tranqued too long already, dab some scent-blocker under her nostrils before she wakes up. By the time it wears off they'll smell right again."

"That's a better plan," says the vet, exchanging nods with the keepers.

"Yes," agrees Christine, the lady keeper. "But I thought there were three chicks?"

"There are. Hand her over, Josh. You can't keep her."

In the night's cold, Gold was keen to get inside my coat again the moment I came back to the cab, and by then the chicks already stank so much of human there wasn't much point refusing her. But I wasn't trying to *keep* her. I mean... "An allo, Uncle Z?" It comes out a bit more sarcastic than I intended. "Oh, *sure* I was gonna *keep* her."

He just gives me a look.

"Okay, okay." Regretfully, I unzip my coat and lift her warm, downy self out. "Here. This one's Gold. She's the tamest. *And* she's been blessed, too."

They're all staring, rather blankly. "Tamest? Obviously," murmurs Christine, faintly. She shakes herself. "Uh, can we get a picture, actually? You and the chicks?"

"Awww, I don't know." I glance at Uncle Z and he glares a bit, wanting me to co-operate with our client. "Oh, c'mon, I don't want to be on some zoo info board, forever..."

"Well..." Christine's face falls, then brightens. "We could just show the chicks, in your coat and on your lap. Not your face. How about that? The public would love a photo like that."

"Well...I guess that would be okay."

Gold gets to go back in my coat for a moment, her head out—super cute—and I settle Frankie and Myrrh on my lap, still wearing their little coats. She's right, the public will go gooey over this shot. The keeper seems to be aiming to leave my face off, like she said, and soon enough it's done.

"Be a good girl, Gold," I tell her, stroking her soft feathers and kissing the top of her head, her familiar scent filling my nose. "You're gonna have a safe, comfortable, quiet life. Nothing's gonna eat you while you're little. And no pack of winter-hungry Utahraptors are gonna pull you down and eat you once you're grown. You're not gonna watch your chicks snatched away by a hundred dangers or get killed by some bigger, meaner female that wants your territory. I don't need to worry about you, do I? It sure was nice knowing you, though."

I hand her to Christine, my throat tight. Gold twists her head to look at me, peeping uncertainly: *Why are you giving me to this complete stranger?* "Ah, come on, Gold, you're a big, tough allo. Don't be like that."

Christine smiles. "We'll look after them, don't worry."

"Yeah, I know."

As the chicks are whisked away into the cabin for a check-up, Uncle Z rests a hand on my shoulder. "Guess we'll have to catch you another rodento'saur some time."

My heart leaps. "Really?"

Uncle Z takes his hand from my shoulder and eyes all the bandages on his fingers. "On second thought—no."

I sigh, though I'm not surprised. Uncle Z did actually give me a rodento'saur after Dad died, to try and cheer me up—and a surprisingly laid-back little pet it made, too. But it was too curious for its own good—squeezed into the rear pen a couple of months ago and got stepped on by a young armadillion. Generally, though, he's not a fan of sharing the 'Vi with anything that has sharp teeth unless it's locked safely away in the rear pen or the critter cages.

We climb up to the obsoDeck and stand there under a starry sky—badly marred by all the city-lights—watching Star slumbering in the pen as we wait for our money to arrive in our account.

"Dad would've really liked all this," I say at last. "Saving Star, taming the chicks, meeting that priest again. Right?"

Uncle Z's silent for a long time. "Yeah," he says at last. "Yeah, he would." And he slips his arm around me and holds me close. It makes my ribs twinge, but I don't care.

"And he'd've done the same as you did," he says, softly.

Warmth fills my sore chest. Again I hear Father Ben saying, "He looks real like him." It makes me happy to think how like Dad I am. Uncle Z likes our life, sure enough, but he don't love critters quite the way Dad and I do.

Uncle Z sighs. "Heck," he murmurs, "why'd I go and say that? Now you'll think you did the right thing. I'd've shaken him for it too, y'know?"

"You sure would." I can just see it.

His grip on my shoulder tightens. "Be more careful, Josh. I've this selfish desire to be reunited with Isaiah before you—senior's prerogative, y'know? And if I let it happen the other way around, it'll sure be an awkward reunion."

"Yeah, yeah. Don't be in too much of a rush." The thought of Uncle Z dying as well sends an icy lump sliding down my spine. He'd be with Dad—but I'd be all alone.

Just as he'd be now if Star had eaten me... Huh. After a moment, I add, "I will *try* not to do it again."

"Only try, huh? I'd say for such a young man, you know yourself rather well."

I shrug. His grip tightens again, but he doesn't say anything more, just lets his head rest against mine.

Soon enough, a keeper calls up that our money's gone through—and we're done. We head down from the obsoDeck. Even here, in the comparative openness of the zoo-park, the city looms around me in the darkness, smothering, crushing, choking me.

"Uncle Z?" I say, as we get back into the 'Vi.

"Josh?"

"Do we have to go to the 'Vi-park? We're not due to

re-supply yet; can't we just head straight out again?"

Uncle Z says nothing for a few moments, looking at me in that way that says he's thinking we should stay in-city for a few days to work on my phobia. But, finally, he smiles. "Ah, what the heck, it's Christmas. Let's get out of here and have some fun."

My heart soars, even the ache in my chest seeming to lessen. "What, ain't you been having fun this Christmas, Uncle Z?" I tease.

"Ha ha."

"Y'mean *ho ho*, right?" I settle in my seat and fasten my lap belt to spare my ribs.

"I mean *ho ho, let's go*."

I guess we're a little hysterical with relief. But we laugh like chuckle'saurs as we drive out of the city, away from all the lights, making one lame joke after another, then pull off in the first quiet spot to put the kettle on and cook the first hot food we've had in hours. The 'Vi's a real mess, though.

"Just take some pain pills," says Uncle Z, when we've eaten, "shower and go to bed. We can tidy up in the morning. Come to think of it, I have something for you. Ah, well—tomorrow."

I've got something for him too, come to that. It *is* Christmas. Tomorrow. When we're rested.

Despite my tiredness I'm feeling pretty dang good as I settle into my sleeping bag, clean and full-bellied, with the fire in my chest and back finally starting to die down as the pills kick in. We're alive and well. Star's alive and well. The chicks are alive and well. The little family Saint Des entrusted to us is still together. Despite all the pain and fear and stress, it *has* been a good Christmas.

Weird, but good.

And it ain't over yet.

==+==

You can make a difference!

Reviews and recommendations are vital to any author's success. If you liked this book, please write a short review—a few lines are enough—and tell your friends about the book too.
You will help the author to create new stories and allow others to share your enjoyment.

Your support is important. Thank you.

DON'T MISS

PLEASE DON'T FEED THE DINOSAURS

IN A JURASSIC FUTURE, SOME STILL CHOOSE FREEDOM—DESPITE THE DANGERS.

It takes more than a T. rex scratching its back on his Habitat Vehicle to alarm young hunter Joshua—he's used to living close to nature. But a routine visit to the zoo to deliver a new velociraptor turns deadly when he comes face-to-face with an eleven-foot allosaur called Gold. He knew her when she was a tiny chick—is he a friend from the past—or dinner?

Meanwhile, Darryl and her brother, Harry, are taken completely by surprise when their father remarries. Their new step-mom is a glamorous fashion designer who's never been outside the city's electric fences. How will she cope with a life of dinosaur farming? All Darryl can do is try to get her new stepmom safely to the farm. But once you're unSPARKed, things don't always go to plan...

PLEASE NOTE: Please Don't Feed the Dinosaurs knits together the original unSPARKed book 1, DRIVE!, with the short story 'A Dino Whisperer at the Zoo,' along with a small amount of original material.

OUT NOW!
Read on for a SNEAK PEEK!

"Tell that hunter-boy to hurry up. I haven't got all day," snaps the man in the suit.

I glance out at the welcome party that stands on the obsoDeck. Ned Greyson, stocky and light-skinned, is Exception City Zoo's Head Raptor Keeper. I know him moderately well—the Wilson HabVi has supplied quite a few critters to this zoo over the years. The young Hispanic man—older than me but with that wet-behind-the-ears air most city-boys have—is an eager young underling, or intern, or some-such. The pretty lady—of Cheyenne heritage, I think—is the zoo vet. And there's the thin, pale man in a suit, looking down his nose at everyone, but especially at me in my camo-jacket and heavy boots. He hasn't even spoken to me. Keeps passing things through Ned.

Ned doesn't 'tell me' anything, he just screws up his face in apology and opens his hand in a 'let it go' gesture. He needn't worry. The guy's getting my goat but it takes more than that to blow my fuse.

"There we go." As Silky the velociraptor finally steps off my Habitat Vehicle's ramp into the zoo's holding pen, I press the button to lift the ramp and seal the rear door. He skitters away nervously, but by the time I've dropped out of the HabVi and climbed up to the obsoDeck to join the group standing looking down into the pen, he's run back up to the rear of the large grey vehicle where it's parked flush with the gateway, begging to be let back in, peeping plaintively like he's a juvenile again. "Sorry, Silky," I tell him, raising my voice. "This is your new home, now."

I ignore Suit-man and speak to Ned. "Yep, one velociraptor, male, adult, and zoo-tame."

Silky scratches at the 'Vi with one wing-arm claw, shoots a nervous look around at the strange pen, then calls pathetically.

"Ready to mate?" queries Ned, a twinkle in his eye.

I grin. "Yep. Though he ain't cutting a very manly figure this moment, is he? Too much new."

Ned grins too, but he looks pleased. Silky is young and healthy, virtually adult size—as tall as a wolf and several times longer from nose to tail tip—and into his adult plumage, his unusually soft, sleek charcoal grey feathers set off nicely by his dark blue ruff. A real beauty, and a perfect zoo animal.

But Suit-man steps up to the edge of the obsoDeck and peers down, making Silky start and bolt into the farthest corner of the pen. Suit-man frowns. "Well, this raptor doesn't seem very zoo-tame to me. It's terrified of everything."

"What d'you expect? He's never been in a place like this."

"We're paying extra for a raptor that isn't going to cower away from people and make the visitors think we're mistreating it. I've heard of you hunters' tricks. If you're trying to pass off some sub-standard creature on us, you won't get paid at all."

Ned winces and holds up a hand. "Now, Mr. Grundvick—"

But I don't care what Ned plans to say. Suit-man's suspicion is just one slur too many. He's gonna get punched if he keeps treating hunters like this—this guy could try even a hunter's self-restraint. But there are better ways to make a point.

"Not tame, huh?" I take two steps to the edge of the obsoDeck.

"Aw, heck, Joshua, don't you—"

I ignore Ned—and drop lightly down into the pen.

DARRYL

After knocking back my last swig of coffee, I slip on my denim jacket and pause on my way to the gun locker, checking my reflection in the hall mirror. Shoulder-length brown hair brushed—and loose, for once—face clean, blue eyes...glum. But this has happened, whether I like it or not, so I might as well make a good first impression.

"Harry, get down here, we're going to be late!"

The volume of Dad's latest bellow up the stairs shows that he means business. Well, *I'm* ready, at least.

I thought my younger brother had come around to the 'might as well make a good impression' viewpoint as well, but there's still no noise from upstairs. The fact is, when your dad comes back from a routine weekend market and supply trip to the city and announces that he's got honest-to-God *married* and that the woman—sorry, step-mom—will be coming to live with you, three weeks really isn't enough time to deal with it.

Harry totally lost it. Screamed Lord knows what at Dad, then ran off to the nearest barn. I managed not to do any screaming, but I had to go up and shut myself in the farmhouse's observation turret for almost an hour, and talk to myself *a lot*. You know: *Dad's been alone a long time, Darryl; if he's fallen in love that's wonderful, isn't it, Darryl; you want your father to be happy, don't you, Darryl?*

He totally sprung it on us, though. I guess he was so scared Potential Step-Mom—sorry, Carol—would come to her senses and decide that no handsome, propertied man of her own age was worth going and living unSPARKed on some farm. Carol's a city girl, all right.

When I finally managed to go back down and say something about being happy for Dad and try to show some interest in his new bride, he showed me a photo on his phone, and my heart didn't lift. Just sank even further. Manicured Carol looked like she'd never got within a mile of the city fence in her life, let alone stepped outside it. A less likely farmer's wife I had never seen.

Dad could tell what I was thinking, of course. Brain not completely scrambled by love. "I know Carol's no farmer, Darryl my girl," he told me, "but really, it doesn't matter, does it? We've run the farm by ourselves all this time. She can run her fashion design and consultancy business from the house—I'm getting a faster Net connection put in. And *we'll* run the farm, just as before. And you and Harry will inherit it, Darryl, no question. Carol has her own money."

I reach the gun locker and place my hand on the scanner. Much as I hated to hear Dad talking about *his will*, it's a relief to know the farm is safe. I could put up with a harem of step-moms if I had to, but if someone took the farm from me...

As I take my rifle from the rack I can't help smiling at the thought of Dad with a *harem* of Carols. No, not Dad. We're Catholic, you know. One spouse at a time. Carol's 'not religious,' apparently. I hope that won't matter. Dad did say he thinks she's 'open to it' so that's something.

I throw my ammunition sash on and check the pouches. Three hold full mags, but since we'll be traveling unSPARKed...I'll add the fourth pouch. I put my hand on the scanner to open the ammo box and take a handful of HiPiRs, or Hide Piercing Rounds. Penetrate any hide up to T. rex, these will. Though for T. rex, I really would prefer a bigger gun. *Much* bigger.

"HARRY!" roars Dad, then heads over to me. "Whoa, girl, wait up. Come on, put the rifle away."

"What?" I turn an incredulous look on him. "We're travelling unSPARKed, Dad."

"Carol's nervous enough about the trip as it is, let alone living out here. If we turn up looking like Rambo-family, she's going to freak out. I'll have my rifle. Leave yours here. Just this once."

"But why have one rifle when you can have three?" I demand.

"Most people don't take *any* weapons when they travel, Darryl."

"*City* people. And sometimes when they break down or crash, they get eaten."
"Come on, Darryl, just this once. It will make Carol feel so much better."

Dad's pleading tone is too much. I unsling my rifle from my shoulder and put it back in its place. "All right. But we'd better not end up Raptor Food."

"Of course we won't." He sounds downright cheerful with relief.

JOSHUA

"Hey, Silky-boy." I move out into the middle of the small space and drop into a crouch, making myself smaller and non-threatening as I pull a training treat from my pocket. One knee I keep bent, blocking access to my stomach, while I tuck my left wrist under my chin, palm inwards, shielding my neck. Zoo-tame ain't all the way tame, not by a long shot. "Hey, Silky-boy, Mr. Suit thinks you ain't tame enough for his liking. Poor Silky-boy. Come on, then..."

"Joshua, just come out of there," urges Ned, in a low voice.

I ignore him, too busy saying friendly things in velociraptor-speak, though I need hardly bother. Silky is already running eagerly towards me, drawn as much by my familiarity as by the treat. When he pauses a few feet away, his head on the same level as mine since I'm crouched down, I toss him the meaty drop and pull out another one. He advances again, more confidently. When he's almost close enough to grab for it, I toss it into his mouth. "Good boy. Not scared of humans, are you? Just scared of new."

He takes the last few steps and rubs his head against me, like a hatchling begging a parent for food. Yes, he's very nervous of the strange place, and it's making him even friendlier than usual.

Crooning reassuringly like an adult to a chick—but

keeping my knee and left wrist firmly in place—I stroke his charcoal grey back, healthy young velociraptor scent filling my nostrils. When he just carries on nudging me with his head and peeping anxiously, I slide an arm around him in a hug and ruffle his breast feathers, then glance at Mr. Suit.

"So, mister," I ask him, Silky's teeth inches from my face, "is this raptor tame enough for your liking?"

Get PLEASE DON'T FEED THE DINOSAURS from your favorite retailer today!

The Boy Who Knew

FRIENDS IN HIGH PLACES: CARLO ACUTIS

DEAD? DEFINE DEAD.

"You have leukemia."

Daniel's just received the worst news a teen can get. The adults in his life are crumbling under the shock. In desperation, he turns to his parish priest for help and is introduced to a boy his age, Carlo Acutis—who just happens to be dead.

Daniel's convinced the priest is wasting his time. But as he struggles to come to terms with his uncertain future an unlikely friendship develops between him and the holy dead boy—who may not be quite so dead after all.

The Boy Who Knew is the first title in Carnegie Medal nominee Corinna Turner's new 'Friends in High Places' series. If you've always been interested in the saints but find dry biographies boring and hard to get through, this fast-paced story is for you.

"Powerful and inspiring."
SUSAN PEEK, author of the God's Forgotten Friends series

"beautifully honest"
KARINA FABIAN,
author of *Discovery*

READ ON FOR A SNEAK PEEK

"You have leukemia."

I keep seeing the doctor's eyes over his mask, darting from me to my parents. I keep hearing his words in my head. Mum burst into tears. Dad started pounding on the doctor's desk with his fists. Me, I just sat there.

Leukemia. How can I have leukemia? I'm fifteen. Stuff that bad doesn't happen to people my age, right?

But the tiredness... The bruising...

"You have leukemia."

When we got home from the hospital, Mum started getting ready for the Vigil Mass as usual. Dad never comes along, these days, but tonight...tonight he started yelling at Mum *how could she possibly think there was a God if He could let this happen to me? How could she think He was good?* And Mum shouted back that *God was my only hope, couldn't he see that? Did he want me to die?*

They were still screaming at each other when I slipped out of the house and walked to church. I don't think I've ever come to church on my own before. I felt really self-conscious. Any other week I'd have grabbed the chance to skip Mass. Today, I am angry with God, I suppose? But I'm also really, really scared. And I just wanted to escape the shouting.

Mum never showed up for Mass. I got a text during the first reading: *Daniel, where are you?* I texted back: *At church.* An old lady glared at me over the top of her un-environmentally friendly single-use mask.

Then I fell asleep during the homily. I'm just so tired all the time. I got glared at again.

Now everyone's gone, and I'm still sitting here. I'm afraid to go home in case they're still arguing. Or in case they want to talk about it all. I feel numb. I haven't even taken my mask off, though I'm alone.

"You have leukemia."

"Do you want Daniel to die?"

Am I going to die? Words from one of the readings I heard before I nodded off come into my mind: *There is no need to worry; but if there is anything you need, pray for it.*

"God, please don't let me die," I whisper.

God doesn't reply. Maybe Dad's right. Pulling my mask of at last, I shove it into my pocket, hands shaking.

"God, I'm scared."

Nothing. Well, except that the numbness shatters and, suddenly, I really *feel* the fear, turning my belly into a black hole, cold as a...a...a morgue?

I bury my face in my hands as the sobs rip from me. *Am I going to die, Lord?*

Distant footsteps from the front of the church.

They pause, then tread briskly along the aisle. Towards me. Oh no.

I wipe my face, desperately trying to stop the gasping, heaving sobs. Snot smears my sleeve. Yuck.

"Hi, Daniel."

Reluctantly, I glance up, my shoulders still shuddering. It's Father Thomas. He's young and kinda cool, sweeping around in his long black dress—sorry, *cassock*—without a trace of embarrassment. I wish I had his total lack of self-consciousness.

"Hi, Father." My voice wobbles. *Play it cool, Daniel. Just pretend you're fine and get up and leave.*

"Are you okay?"

"No." I'm shaking my head. What happened to leaving? And then I'm blurting, "I've got leukemia."

His lips part as though I just punched him in the gut. "Oh, Daniel…" He settles into the next wide-spaced pew, sitting sideways to face me, eyes narrowed in concern. "Heck, I thought you were going to say bullying or something. That's a hard thing to face, at your age. When are you starting treatment? Did they say…what the prognosis is?"

"Prognosis?" I sound like an idiot. Oh, whether I'm going to live or die, he means. "Oh, uh…well, I just got the preliminary test result today. After more tests on Monday morning, the specialists make a plan and I see them the next Monday and…well, that's when they'll tell me…y'know. They think I'll start treatment almost at once."

"That's good. Just time for a novena, too."

"What?"

He pulls out his wallet and flicks through several business cards before pulling one out. "This is the saint for you. Well, a Blessed, technically. In fact, he's not a Blessed until next Saturday, so I shouldn't really be giving these new cards out yet, but under the circumstances. Here. Almost-Blessed Carlo Acutis. He had leukemia when he was fifteen. Best prayer buddy you could have right now. I think there's a novena on his website."

He sees my vague look. "A novena's when you team up with a saint for nine days to pray for something."

"Oh yeah, I remember." I accept the card and slip it into my pocket, though I'm not sure I want it. Now the numbness has gone, I am starting to feel pretty mad at God. Isn't He supposed to love me? A wire of white-hot rage tightens painfully around my insides, and I scowl towards the tabernacle. Dad's right, how could He let this happen to me? What did I ever do to Him?

"Have you ever made a pot?" asks Father Thomas, suddenly. "Or a painting?"

What? "Uh, I make 3D art on my computer. Loads of it."

"Ah, that's right. I knew you were an artist of some kind. Say if you created a 3D pot, then. Did anyone force you to make it?"

I look at him blankly. "No. I just do it because I want to."

"Could you, like, virtually smash it?"

"In my program? Sure. More or less." A surge of happiness flows through me at the thought of my state-of-the-art 3D design program and extensive inventory of quality assets...then wilts. What good will it all do me if I can't beat this thing?

"Could you take the pieces of your ex-pot and make

them into a mosaic that was far, far more beautiful?"

"If I wanted to."

"And that would be okay? Breaking your pot and remaking it into something better?"

"Of course. It's my pot. I made it, right?"

"And then you could keep your beautiful mosaic forever, right?"

Forever? I may not have a *year*, for all I know... Belatedly, I figure out what he's on about. "Oh, very clever! I'm not a *pot!* It's not the same!"

"No, it's not the same," Father Thomas agrees, unperturbed. "We're far, far more important to God than some 3D pot. Or even a real one. He loves every single hair on our heads—and he knows exactly how many there are."

"Great!" I snap, leaping up from the pew and storming away from his infuriating calm. I yell over my shoulder, "I'll be sure to remember that when they start falling out!"

But I catch his soft words, just before I slip through the door.

"I hope you do."

**Get THE BOY WHO KNEW from
your favorite retailer today!**

ABOUT THE AUTHOR

Corinna Turner has been writing since she was fourteen and likes strong protagonists with plenty of integrity. Although she spends as much time as possible writing, she cannot keep up with the flow of ideas, for which she offers thanks—and occasional grumbles!—to the Holy Spirit. She is the author of over twenty-five books, including the Carnegie Medal Nominated I Am Margaret series, and her work has been translated into four languages. She was awarded the St. Katherine Drexel award in 2022.

She is a Lay Dominican with an MA in English from Oxford University and lives in the UK. She is a member of a number of organizations, including the Society of Authors, Catholic Teen Books, Catholic Reads, the Angelic Warfare Confraternity, and the Sodality of the Blessed Sacrament. She used to have a Giant African Land Snail, Peter, with a 6½" long shell, but now makes do with a cactus and a campervan.

Get in touch with Corinna...

Facebook: Corinna Turner

Twitter: @CorinnaTAuthor

Don't forget to sign up for

NEWS
&
FREE SHORT STORIES
at:

www.UnSeenBooks.com

All Free/Exclusive content subject to availability.

www.ingramcontent.com/pod-product-compliance
Lightning Source LLC
Chambersburg PA
CBHW030754190726
48285CB00003B/844